OF MICE AND MAGIC

OF MICE AND MAGIC

David Farland

DAVID FARLAND

Covenant Communications, Inc.

Cover and interior illustrations © Howard Lyon.
Cover and book design by Jessica A. Warner.
Cover design © 2005 by Covenant Communications, Inc.

Published by Covenant Communications, Inc.
American Fork, Utah

Copyright © 2005 by Dave Farland

All rights reserved. No part of this book may be reproduced in any format or in any medium without the written permission of the publisher, Covenant Communications, Inc., P.O. Box 416, American Fork, UT 84003. This work is not an official publication of The Church of Jesus Christ of Latter-day Saints. The views expressed within this work are the sole responsibility of the author and do not necessarily reflect the position of The Church of Jesus Christ of Latter-day Saints, Covenant Communications, Inc., or any other entity.

This is a work of fiction. The characters, names, incidents, places, and dialogue are products of the author's imagination, and are not to be construed as real.

Printed in Canada
First Printing: October 2005

11 10 09 08 07 06 05   10 9 8 7 6 5 4 3 2 1

ISBN1-57734-918-0

For Spencer Wolverton,
who is always nice to mice.

With special thanks to those who helped in the original brainstorming sessions for the series, including Daniel Wells, Melva Gifford, Lareena Smith, Kristy Merrill, Claudine Swenson, Lisa Hilton, Matt Jones, Barbara Abbott, Ethan & Christy Skaarstedt, Mary Jo Tansy, Dennis Lynn, Matt Hamby, Gina Groeger, and special thanks to Carolyn Larsen.

TABLE OF CONTENTS

Suddenly, a light streaked overhead, a flaming yellow ball that struck Bald Hill.

CHAPTER I

MINOR MIRACLES

Miracles occur right under our snouts every day.
We just don't look closely enough to see them.
—Rufus Flycatcher

BENJAMIN RAVENSPELL'S MOTHER liked to put things off. She never paid her taxes until the tax agents beat down her door. She could go months without mopping. And she never bothered to cook dinner—period. Instead, she'd just waste away until her hunger drove her to throw Ben in the car and race to the nearest fast food restaurant.

Which is how nine-year-old Benjamin Ravenspell found himself eating at McDonald's at midnight on Christmas Eve.

The speaker overhead played "Silent Night" as Ben's mom scarfed down Chicken McNuggets and asked, "So, honey, what would you like Santa to bring you tomorrow?"

Finally, Ben thought. He'd been waiting weeks for her to ask that question, but she had put it off and put it off and put it off—as usual.

"Mmmph." Ben tried to clear a french fry from his throat. "I want a pet!"

His mom's eyes widened in surprise, and her face went as red as a pomegranate. She coughed up a McNugget. It arced over the table and plopped onto some bald guy's neck. The fellow grabbed it, eyed it suspiciously, and then plopped it in his mouth as if it were manna from heaven.

"But, but," she sputtered, "I thought you wanted a baby brother!"

Ben thought back. He had wanted one last year on his birthday, but that was forever ago.

"Not anymore," Ben said.

"What if it's too late to change your mind?" his mom shouted, growing hysterical.

Ben knew that he wouldn't get a pet for Christmas. His mom probably already had a baby hidden in her closet. All she'd have to do is wrap it in gold paper and shove it under the tree.

Ben explained, "Colton, who lives down the street, asked for a baby brother—and the doctor gave him a *sister!* All she does is stink up diapers and suck on stuff. She leaves a slime trail wherever she goes. The kids call her the 'Rug Slug.'"

"Okay," his mom said, as if trying to think of some way to change his mind. "What kind of pet would you like? You know that I'm allergic to cats and dogs."

Ben thought. "Could I get a mammoth?"

"Mammoths are just pretend, hon."

"Well, I want something cool. I want a pet that I can play with and talk to, one that will be my friend—"

"We'll have to think about that," she said, which was her way of putting him off.

As he tried to sleep that night, Ben heard his mom and dad downstairs under the Christmas tree. Ben always took a football helmet and baseball bat to bed, just in case a monster invaded his closet. So he took off his football helmet, laid his baseball bat by his bed, and sneaked to the top of the stairs.

"What are we going to do?" Mom asked Dad. "We've tried for a baby for months. Now he's changed his mind."

"I'm glad he changed his mind," Dad said. "If we had a baby tomorrow, he'd get bored with it in a week—and we'd be stuck with *another* kid."

Ben inched to the landing and peered through the banister rails. His mom and dad knelt under the Christmas tree. Mom had never taken the tree down. It had been sitting in the corner since last year and had gathered so much dust, it looked as if it was covered in gray snow. Cobwebs seemed to be holding it upright.

"Ben needs a friend," she said. "Ever since Christian . . . he's been . . . lost."

Ben felt a pang. Christian had been his best friend. Then Christian's dad got a job at a penguin cannery in Antarctica, and the whole family moved away.

"What's he need friends for?" Dad asked. "I never had any, and I turned out all right."

"I had a friend, once," Mom said. "You have to have a friend to learn how to be a friend."

"He'll never have a friend," Dad objected. "At his age, there are only two kinds of kids—jocks and nerds. Ben isn't either."

"He's a jock, definitely," Mom said. "He's almost got his black belt in karate."

"He's a wimp," Dad objected. "You can only be a real jock if your knuckles drag the ground. Besides, he reads books, for heaven's sake! What kind of weird kid reads books?"

Dad's right, Ben thought. *Most kids specialize in something. You could only be a friend with a jock like Spencer Grimes if you could hawk boogers across the playground. And you could only be friends with a nerd like T. J. Piddly if you had all gazillion Yu-Gi-Oh! cards.*

But Christian had been the kind of friend you could jump puddles with or explore sewers with or just talk to. Friends like that were hard to find.

"Ben needs to learn how to get by without friends," Dad concluded. "Maybe if we could make him grow up faster, get through this awkward phase. Maybe we could try steroids. In a couple of years, we could turn that runt into a grunt. He'll make plenty of friends when he joins the Marines."

"You know," Mom said, "Ben has a birthday coming up in a couple of months . . ."

"Well," Dad said, "He's not ready for a pet. He'd have to feed it and clean its cage. Any kid who doesn't keep his room clean isn't ready to have a pet."

Humph, Ben thought. *By Dad's way of thinking, Mom would never be ready to have a kid!*

The truth was, Ben didn't have any friends because his mom never cleaned the house. At school, they said that it was so dirty that you had to wipe your shoes *after* you left. They called it the Roach Hotel. No one ever wanted to come over, and Ben figured that if he got any less popular, even his imaginary friends would start avoiding him.

"All right," Mom said. "We'll tell him tomorrow. If Ben can prove that he can be responsible, we'll take him to Noah's Ark and let him pick out a pet."

"What kind?" Dad asked. "A guppy or a gorilla?"

"A *small* pet," Mom said.

So Ben went to bed, and in his dreams, a talking rabbit took him fishing for perch on the Long Tom River. The perch lay big and purple under the water, like bruises, burping.

A duck with a dozen chicks swam by, warning her young, "Be careful, those hooks can put out your eye."

When Ben tried to put a worm on his hook, it wriggled away crying, "Why can't I be your pet? I'm not as slimy as a little sister!"

And if darker dreams disturbed his slumber, Ben did not recall them in the morning.

* * *

Ben's mom and dad didn't talk to him about the pet on Christmas morning, but Ben thought about it all the time. He cleaned his room that day, and when his mom took him to town later that week, he stopped at Noah's Ark and peered through the windows at the hamsters.

He tried very hard to start growing, so that his dad would like him better, and he only read in secret. In an effort to make some friends, he tried smiling and being friendly, even to the weirdest kids at school, but no one wanted to be his friend.

* * *

On the thirteenth night of the thirteenth month of the new millennium, Ben sensed a change. He could feel it in the wind and wondered at it even as he dressed for bed. Something was different. He could almost smell . . . magic in the air.

All day long, snow had fallen. Lazy flakes drifted into heaps, settling between the fir trees in his backyard. Then the clouds fled and stars simmered in the sky, casting a web of silvery light on the snow, while the moon sprung up as orange as a pumpkin.

The neighbors still had their Christmas lights on, winking from the eaves. And in the backyard, a snowman leaned over, almost as if it bent to pick up the carrot nose that had fallen from its face.

Suddenly, a light streaked overhead, a flaming yellow ball that struck Bald Hill, exploding in a blaze of glory.

"Look, a star fell!" Ben told his mom, who was staring in awe at the clean sheets that Ben had starched and ironed and put on his bed that morning.

"Make a wish," she said.

Ben's heart hammered. He let his mind drift, as if it were seeking across the world to connect to the object of his desire. Then he whispered, "I wish I had a pet—uh, I mean a friend. I mean a friendly pet."

He put on the football helmet that he kept by his nightstand, grabbed his baseball bat, and jumped into bed.

"You know," his mom said, "other children sleep with teddy bears to help them feel safe."

"Don't be silly," Ben said. "If a robber broke in, hitting him with a teddy bear wouldn't help. Would it?"

"I suppose not." She sighed. It was an old argument. Ben had slept with his bat and helmet for years. "I guess that I should be grateful that you don't want to keep swords in your bed."

Ben said his prayers, and his mom gave him a peck on the cheek, wished him "Good night," and slipped from his room.

* * *

And outside, miracles occurred.

Thirteen minutes after the first star fell, another streaked through the sky at a perfect twenty-degree angle to its left. And every thirteen minutes, another star fell, until thirteen had fallen in all, each aligned perfectly with the thirteen cardinal points on the compass—at least as cardinal points are understood by crows.

And in Dallas, Oregon, small wonders broke out everywhere, though no one—at least no humans—took notice.

Thirteen dazed children suddenly put aside their video games and rushed to do homework. Thirteen mutts began to howl so beautifully that the nuns at St. Mary's thought that it was a heavenly choir announcing the Second Coming. In Ben's backyard, the snowman leaned over, picked up the carrot, screwed it onto his face, and trudged away.

While at Noah's Ark Pet Shop, the greatest wonder of all occurred. Beneath the pale light thrown by the fish tanks that held the neon tetras, a mother mouse gave birth.

Twelve small, pink kittens she had in her nest, all with eyes closed. The other mice gathered in awe. Even the angelfish across the room gaped with eyes as bright as gold coins.

The lights above the fish tanks flashed brightly, and their green glow came together to form something that lived and breathed. Thirteen luna moths appeared, circling above the mouse pen like a crown, their pale green wings flapping in unison, their graceful tails sweeping behind. The feeder crickets at the front counter began to fiddle beautifully as the thirteenth mouse made its way, squeaking and squirming, into the world.

As it dropped into the wood shavings, a wise old mouse named Barley Beard said reverently, "Thirteen, and the last is a girl—just as the prophets foretold. A thirteenth miracle on this night of miracles."

"But Grandfather," a young mouse asked, "what's so special about *this* mouse?"

Barley Beard said, "I only know that the number thirteen is normally unlucky, and in some ways this kit is destined to lead a dangerous life, for her enemies will seek to destroy her. Yet on this night of nights, all of the fortune in the world will flow into this child."

"You mean she'll be lucky?" the young one asked.

"More than lucky—she'll be magic! Not since we small creatures ruled the earth has a mouse like this been born." Barley Beard peered at the glass walls of his cage, longing to escape. He didn't need to remind the young ones that to be born in a cage was hard indeed. No mouse of the field could be born to a more humble fate.

Barley Beard only hoped that the young kit would find a way to free them all.

A shadow darkened the window, and Barley Beard glanced outside. A snowman plodded past, dressed in a fine top hat, twirling a cane.

Odd, Barley Beard thought, as he watched the man of snow waddle under the streetlight, ice crystals glittering like diamonds. But soon the snowman was gone. He trudged several blocks, until he found a snowgirl in a yard nearby. Then he cuddled against her, one arm wrapped over her shoulder, and waited for spring.

He finally noticed one mouse that was different, the smallest of the lot, sitting in the shavings.

CHAPTER 2

THE CAGE

Everyone lives in a cage.
Sometimes the cage is made by others, but mostly
we live in cages built by the limits of our imaginations.
—RUFUS FLYCATCHER

BEN'S MOM AND DAD NEVER MENTIONED the pet again. Still, Ben did his best to show that he could be responsible.

Every afternoon, he cleaned his room when he got home from school. He pushed the vacuum cleaner over the floor so much that he sucked fibers out of the carpet. Thus his room became an island of neatness in a sea of chaos, and his mother worried about his strange behavior so much that she went so far as to think about calling a psychiatrist.

But of course, like everything else, she put it off.

After cleaning, Ben practiced karate and did homework. When he ran out of homework, he made up math problems and solved them. He wrote essays on how to take care of pets he'd like to own—from anteaters to a T-Rex.

He did so much homework that at the end of a week, his teachers sent angry notes to his parents. "Don't you think I have better things to do than correct papers all night?" bleated his English teacher, Mrs. Lamb. "Give me a break!" grunted his history teacher, Mr. Hogg. "Get a life!" howled his math teacher, Mrs. Vixen.

But no matter how much homework Ben did, he couldn't impress his parents.

So a week before his birthday, he came home with a plan. "Mom," he said, "this kid from school, Hakim, is going to New York for a couple of weeks, and he said that he'd pay me ten dollars if I'd take care of his lizard. Can I babysit his lizard?"

His mother grew suspicious. Ten dollars seemed like a fortune just for taking care of a lizard. She knew that you should never trust a deal that sounded too good to be true. "Well, do you know how to take care of it?"

"Hakim said it's easy. The lizard hardly eats a thing. He wrote directions!" Ben handed the note to his mom. Hakim was in fifth grade, so he'd written in cursive, which Ben had a hard time with. And everything that Hakim wrote looked suspiciously like Arabic. Ben couldn't figure out what the squiggly marks meant.

As his mother read, her face paled, and her hand began to tremble. She asked, "Can you handle this?"

"You bet!" Ben said. What better way was there to prove that he could take care of a pet than to do it?

So that night, Hakim brought the lizard. It was a Nile monitor, nearly black with sandy yellow stripes on its tail and gorgeous yellow spots on its legs and back. At nearly three feet long, it was a monster!

* * *

For her first few weeks, the thirteenth mouse lay weak and scrawny. Her pink skin had no hair, and she shivered most of the time. Being born blind, she couldn't see where to find food, and her larger brothers and sisters shoved her aside at feedings so that she got almost nothing to eat.

She grew weaker and weaker until she was too weary to even shiver. Barley Beard feared that she would die.

So he nuzzled up to her, pushing her tiny body with his nose so that he could urge her toward her mother. The kitten was too weak to crawl.

Barley Beard whispered urgently, "Live, darn you. Live!"

And in a faint voice, the baby mouse asked, "Why? Dying would be so much easier."

"Because we need you," Barley Beard said. "I need you. Your mother and brothers and sisters all need you."

"What for?" the babe managed to ask.

Barley Beard wasn't sure how to answer. "We live in a cage," Barley Beard said at last. "The walls around us are invisible, but they are thick and real, and there is no getting past them."

"Who holds us here?"

"Strange creatures called humans. They are like pinkies—no fur except for a little on their heads."

"Can't you bite these pinkies?" the babe asked.

"The pinkies are enormous. They're a hundred times taller than a mouse and a thousand times fatter. We cannot fight them. We are powerless."

"Why?" the baby mouse asked weakly. "Why do they want us here?"

"From time to time, the big pinkies take us from our prison. Some say that they love us and that when they take us, they embrace us—they usher us to their havens, where we are pampered and fed exotic foods. In the havens, the wood shavings are piled deep and every mouse has a warm corner where he can lie down in his own nest. There are running wheels and other toys to play with, and when you tire of them, the big pinky children preen you and cuddle you and give you the love that you deserve."

By now, the other mice had gathered around to listen. They circled Barley Beard and his ailing charge.

"It sounds wonderful," one young mouse said. "Why would she want to save us from that?"

"Because," Barley Beard said, "there is something better than being embraced. There is something called *freedom*."

He turned from the young mouse that had spoken, and studied the babe. She was small, blind, hairless, and too weak to move. "Once, long ago, another mouse came here a—wild mouse—who scurried under the pet shop door. He told about life beyond the cage, life away from the big pinkies, in a sunny place called the Endless Meadow. It lies just outside the pet shop, he said. It is a place that the Great Master of Field and Fen created just for mice. There food grows untamed atop the tall grasses, and all you have to do is shake a hay stalk, and grain tumbles to the ground. There, you can drink sweet water from dewdrops that cling to the clover. There, he said, beautiful wildflowers tower overhead in a riot of color. Wild peas grow thick among the fields, and strawberries lie fat on the vine, just waiting for you to nibble. There, he said, the sky fills with sunlight and rainbows by day, and twinkling stars and crescent moons by night.

"The Endless Meadow," Barley Beard sighed. "I have never seen it, except in dreams. But that is our true home. That is our destiny. And if you will live, little mouse, you can lead us there."

The baby mouse listened, but Barley Beard could not tell if she heard him. Her eyes were cloudy. Most likely, she was off in a dream, and she would slip in and out of it until she starved.

All day long and far into the night, Barley Beard rested beside her, warming her with his own body, nuzzling her tummy so that he could stimulate it to hunger.

He prayed to the Great Master of Field and Fen, begging Him to spare her. And at dawn his prayer was answered. A big pinky, a human woman that the mice called Feeder, came to their pens, humming an ancient tune. She carried away six blind kittens.

"Hooray," the kittens cried as Feeder lifted them. "We're being embraced. Good-bye. Have a good life!"

So the pet shop mice rejoiced for the young ones. And with them gone, the thirteenth mouse finally had a chance to get some food.

But Barley Beard worried that the relief from hunger came too late. The little one had starved too long. "She's so thin and sickly," he mused, "will she even be able to lift her head to eat?" For though there was now space for her to drink, she was too far gone to crawl to her mother. That night, the young kitten lay as still as a corpse.

Several times in the darkness, Barley Beard felt her chest fall, and then it seemed it did not rise again for a long time. He feared that she had stopped breathing altogether.

But at sunrise, she raised her head once more and began to struggle through the deep wood shavings to her mother's side.

"Go," Barley Beard urged her, tears flowing. "Go now and feed." The other mice cheered, rallying her on, and the thirteenth mouse kicked until she reached her mother.

On that glorious morning she fed.

By the end of her first week, she began to grow. She looked different from other pet shop mice. She wasn't brownish gray like her brothers and sisters.

Instead, her coat came in with a slight yellow tint. Because of her strange color, her mother named her Amber.

And in three weeks, tiny Amber began to play with other pet shop mice.

Now, a week to a mouse is like a year to a human, so Amber grew quickly. Each day, Barley Beard urged her to test her magical powers.

But as far as Barley Beard could tell, Amber had none. "Don't worry," Barley Beard tried to soothe her. "Just put your trust in the Great Master of Field and Fen."

Amber sat for hours that night, snuggled in a corner, peering through the glass wall toward the fish tanks and the frog terrariums. She wondered what purpose her life really served. There was none that she could see.

On the shelf above her, the fancy spotted mice raced about in their elegant mouse habitat, exploring brightly colored tunnels. They often called out, "Wow, I found another yogurt chip in our gourmet feed. Too bad you brown mice don't get any." Then the other spotted mice would laugh and shout down to the brown mice, "Say, why don't you get out of your cage and come up to play on our exercise wheel?"

What will I ever do? Amber wondered. *Is this all that there is to life, burrowing in my wood shavings, trying to find a clean place to sleep?*

She wanted to be special, more special than even a spotted mouse. She wanted to believe old Barley Beard. But it was clear to her that she had no magical powers. She couldn't free herself, much less the rest of mousekind.

* * *

But that morning, Amber's mother was embraced. Barley Beard was taken a day later.

By then, all of Amber's brothers and sisters had gone, and though there were still plenty of pet shop mice in the cage, Amber felt uprooted, completely alone.

She longed to be free of her dull surroundings and only hoped to be embraced.

* * *

All week long, Ben coddled the monitor lizard. He took baths with it and found that the lizard, whose name was Imhotep, loved to dive and thrash his tail. Then Ben would take Imhotep out, dry him with a blow dryer, and they would watch cartoons beneath a special lizard lamp.

Ben made sure that Imhotep got plenty of water to drink and kept him warm.

And late in the afternoon on Ben's birthday, March twenty-sixth, his mom told him, "Hop in the car. We're going to the pet shop."

Though Noah's Ark Pet Shop was only three miles from his home, this was the first time that Ben had ever been allowed to go *inside*. He immediately felt drawn to the hedgehogs that rooted in their sawdust, merrily grunting.

But his mother marched him to the back of the store, handed him a dollar, and said, "Ugh, pick a mouse."

"Which one?" Ben asked.

"Any mouse," his mom said. "Just buy it, and put it in a bag. I don't want to see the horrible thing." She sneezed and covered her nose. "I've got to get away from these cats before I choke." She took off running.

"A mouse," Ben whispered. "I never thought of getting a mouse."

But it made sense. Dad had said that if he showed that he could be responsible, he could get a *small* pet. And what was smaller than a mouse?

He imagined what fun he could have. He could hold it and pet it and carry it to school in his lunchbox. He'd let it run around his room while he did homework.

It wouldn't eat much, and no one was allergic to mice. A mouse could be a wonderful pet!

Ben peered into the cage. Dozens of fine mice burrowed in the wood shavings, drank at the feeder, or raced around playing tag.

They were plain brown with beady black eyes. A cage nearby had white mice with brown spots, but they were two dollars each. Ben didn't have enough money for a fancy mouse. The ones he looked at were only fifty cents.

He finally noticed one mouse that was different, the smallest of the lot, sitting in the shavings. It had a yellow tinge to its fur, and it folded its paws across its belly. It peered right into Ben's eyes, as if it had been waiting all of its life for Ben to appear.

"May I help you?" a clerk asked, stepping up to him.

"Yes," Ben said. "I want the little one."

* * *

"I'll name it Amber," Ben said in the car. He sat in the back seat with his mouse in its sack. It peered up at him as he petted it with one finger. The mouse sniffed at him, its little whiskers pulling back. Ben didn't know where he got the name Amber. It had just popped into his head.

"I wouldn't get too attached," his mom said as she drove.

"What do you think it eats?" Ben asked. "Would it like pickles? Do we have any pickles in the fridge?"

Mom just kept driving.

"Do you think it's a boy or a girl?" Ben asked.

"I don't think it matters. Just keep it in the sack."

Ben sneaked his mouse out. *His* mouse, his first pet. It climbed up the front of his shirt. It perched in a fold of cloth on his chest and closed its eyes. Ben kissed it.

"Did you just kiss that mouse?" his mom asked, peering at him through the rearview mirror.

"No," Ben lied.

"Never kiss a mouse. They're like rats. Like midget rats. The dirty things carry disease."

"What kinds?" Ben asked, suddenly worried.

"Like the Poopopolous virus and the Black Plague. Now put it back in the sack!"

Ben frowned. He picked up his mouse and hid it in his cupped hand. It didn't look dirty or sick. It just sat with its eyes closed, sleeping. He held still, afraid that the mouse might wake if he moved. Amber rode without making a sound until they got home.

When the car stopped, Ben rushed to the living room where Dad was watching *Samurai Jack*. "Dad, look," Ben called. "I got a mouse, a real mouse. Its name is Amber!"

Dad leaned forward in his chair, eyes on the TV. "Fine," he said in an annoyed tone. "Now march upstairs and feed it to the lizard."

Ben's stomach sank. "Why? What do you mean?"

"You read Hakim's note," Dad said. "You have to feed the lizard once a week."

It seemed to Ben that the heavens opened then. Hakim had said that his lizard didn't eat much, but it had to eat *something*. Of course! Mice. It ate mice!

Ben had never felt so awful. He got sick to his stomach, and the room seemed to sway.

Dad commanded, "Just drop the mouse in the cage. The lizard knows what to do."

"No," Ben pleaded in a small voice. "Please. I . . . can't."

Dad gave him a hard look. "Ben," he said. "You agreed. Imhotep is your responsibility."

"But Dad—"

"Butts," Dad rumbled in his sternest tone, "are for spanking." He pierced Ben with his steely eyes. "Now be a good Marine."

Mom spoke up. "Look, if you go feed *this* mouse to Imhotep, maybe we'll get one for you next week."

Dad gave Mom a sharp look. They hadn't talked about this.

"Really?" Ben asked. "Can I get my own mouse?"

Dad grew angry but said, "Maybe."

"What if . . . what if I keep this one?" Ben asked. "I'll pay you for it with my own allowance." Ben's mom was really lousy at paying allowance. She would put it off and put it off until she owed Ben a small fortune. He figured that right now he had about fifty dollars in back allowance owed to him. "We could go back down to the pet shop and get another mouse," he said eagerly. "That way I could keep Amber."

Dad bayoneted him with a stare. "The pet shop is closed now. The lizard is hungry. Do your duty, *soldier*."

Ben faltered. Dad never called him "soldier" unless he was in deep trouble.

Ben's heart sank. He tried one last desperate plea. "Couldn't we just feed it Spam or something?"

His mom looked up at him and said in a sad voice, "Honey, no one—human or animal—should be forced to eat Spam. That's just too cruel."

Caught between his father's threats and his mother's promise, Ben didn't have a choice.

Cupping Amber in his hand, Ben marched upstairs, lumbering painfully up each step.

As he reached the top, his heart pounded in his ears. He wondered if he dared fake it. Maybe he could hide the mouse under his bed and pretend that he'd fed the lizard.

No, he decided, that would be too dangerous. The lizard might get hungry and die.

He opened his bedroom door.

The beautiful Nile monitor stood regally in his cage, front paws on his sunning log. Imhotep flicked his dark tongue and eyed Ben expectantly. It was as if he'd been waiting for this moment.

Maybe I could give him some candy, Ben thought. He still had some marshmallow chicks in his drawer, leftover from Easter. But that wouldn't do, Ben knew. The lizard ate mice. Candy might make it sick.

Amber huddled in Ben's palm, fast asleep. "I'm sorry," Ben told her. "I'm so sorry."

Amber half woke. The mouse sniffed the air.

Ben couldn't think of anything else to do. He carried Amber to the lizard's cage and slid the screen lid partway open. He took Amber by the tail and lifted her gently.

"Good-bye, Amber," Ben said with quavering lips.

Amber woke. Her dark eyes peered at the lizard. She began squeaking fearfully and wiggled from side to side, swaying as she tried to escape.

The mouse's terror riveted the lizard.

Imhotep flicked his forked tongue, tasting the air, and he stood eagerly with head raised, ready to pounce.

Then something strange happened.

The mouse shrieked louder and louder, until the whole room echoed with its cries.

Ben heard a rumbling sound, like thunder. A blinding blue light flashed.

In an instant, everything changed. Ben shrank out of his clothes, or else his shirt suddenly grew as large as a circus tent. At the same time, something yanked his nose and ears and pinched the skin at the top of his bottom—stretching him in impossible directions. His thumbs shrank to nothing, and his front teeth grew enormous.

Tears of pain blinded Ben.

The mouse was screaming. Screaming.

Ben let out a high shriek.

Amber's tail grew huge. One second, Ben held it between two fingers. The next, he could hardly hold it at all.

He fell with Amber, headfirst, and landed—splat!—right into the deep sand by the lizard's water dish.

Ben blinked. He was no larger than Amber, who sprawled next to him. The glass walls of the cage rose like cliffs around them.

The lizard towered above him too. Ben suddenly knew what it would be like to stare into the face of a hungry dinosaur.

"Allah be praised," the lizard said, flicking his tongue. "Now, if only I had some fava beans and a nice Hawaiian Punch. I love having friends for dinner."

"I'll name it Amber," Ben said in the car.

CHAPTER 3

THE GREAT ESCAPE

No matter how fast you run,
you can't escape your own fear.
The only way to beat it is to face it.
—BUSHMASTER

AMBER BACKED AWAY from the gigantic lizard. Its black tongue snapped like a whip over her head. She stared at Ben in shock. He was absolutely, heartbreakingly, the most handsome mouse she had ever seen!

His onyx eyes mirrored the sparkling light from the lizard lamp. His lustrous pelt had grown a striking reddish gold, darkening until it was nearly black on top. His lithe tail was elegant, dashing. His perfect whiskers made Amber's stomach flip.

"What going on?" Ben asked, blinking. "Who took my thumbs? Where'd I get the mink coat?" He whirled, and his long tail scrambled away behind him. Ben spun, trying to get a good look at it. Suddenly, Amber saw, the truth dawned on him.

"Mom!" Ben screamed, whirling about in a blind panic. "Mom, I've got a problem! I . . . I think I'm a *vermin*!"

The huge lizard, Imhotep, stepped forward. His black tongue stabbed the air above Ben's head. "More than just vermin," Imhotep said in a thick accent. "You're a succulent, full-flavored jumping mouse, if my tongue doesn't deceive me. Firm muscles, well marbled. Just do me a favor: don't squeak on your way down. Hearing my food shriek in my throat really ruins my meal."

"But, but, how did I get this way?" Ben pleaded.

"A curse, of course," Imhotep said. "We invented them in Egypt—mummy's curses, pharaoh's magicians. Why, my own cousin is a genie's apprentice."

"But who cursed me?" Ben wondered.

"The young wizardess." The lizard jutted a chin toward Amber.

Amber's heart pounded. "Me?" Amber squeaked, eyes wide. "*I* zapped him? I can't do magic!"

But someone had turned the boy into a mouse, and Amber knew in her heart that old Barley Beard had been right—she *did* have magical powers!

Ben whirled toward Amber, as if just noticing her. "You're a girl," he shouted. "And I'm naked!" He threw one paw over his chest and crossed his legs.

"Of course you cursed him," Imhotep told Amber in a deep, sedate voice. "You wished that he could see how it feels to be a mouse." He paused, as Amber realized that she had screamed that just as Ben was dropping her into the lizard cage. "Now he's a mouse," Imhotep said with finality. "So, about my dinner . . ."

"Mom!" Ben screamed. His shout echoed off the glass cage, no louder than a mouse's squeak. "The lizard is saying mean things!"

Imhotep lunged.

Amber dove behind a stick. Her fur stood on end. The lizard lamp blazed overhead like a bonfire.

Ben froze with fear for an instant, then stepped back and tripped over his own feet. He crawled behind the lizard's sunning log to hide.

"Wait," Ben called to Imhotep. "Why eat me? I took good care of you!"

"Good care?" Imhotep growled. "You thought I liked watching your favorite cartoons over and over? You thought I liked bubble baths?"

"But," Ben begged, "what about Amber? She's the one you're supposed to eat!"

"Me?" Amber squeaked.

The lizard froze for an instant, as if considering, but suddenly backed away. He was frightened. "I don't like magic mice," the lizard said. "They give me gas."

The lizard stalked forward, angling his body, forcing Ben toward a corner.

Amber looked up and saw that Ben had left the lid halfway open. She got an idea. "Ben,"

Amber shouted. "Jump!" She pointed up to the lid.

"That's got to be fifty feet in the air," Ben screamed. "I can't jump that high. I need a ladder, or a rope . . ."

Amber scampered up the sunning log. In all of her days as a pet shop mouse, she'd never had a stick like this in her cage. She'd never gotten high enough to try to jump out. Now she scaled to the top of the log and leaped an enormous distance. With all of her might, she wished that she could reach the top. She snagged the edge of the lid, clinging by the tips of her paws.

Ben peered up, and saw her tail hanging. "A rope!" Ben said, just as the lizard lunged at him.

His legs seemed to explode beneath him, propelling him up like a marshmallow flipped from a spoon.

He caught Amber's tail and held on for dear life.

"Feeeeed me!" the lizard whined, leaping as best he could and snapping at Ben and Amber. "Feeeeeeed me!"

"Let go of my tail!" Amber shrieked.

"Or what?" Ben asked. "You'll turn me into a slug?"

"Don't tempt me," she shouted.

"Ah," Imhotep said, peering up, "what a sweet delicacy dangles before my eyes! Tastier than the dates at the Temple to Ahmen Ra!"

He climbed up the sunning log and chomped. Ben clung to Amber's tail, screaming and swinging like Tarzan.

"I'm slipping!" Amber cried. Her tiny claws couldn't hold much longer.

"Come down," Imhotep shouted. "I love eating American." He jumped and nipped at Ben.

"Amber," Ben shouted. "Turn the lizard into a bug!"

Amber wondered. *Can I really do that?* But before she could even give it much thought, Ben screamed and kicked off, smashing the lizard on the lips. He must have hit solidly, for Ben went hurtling, and he was still holding Amber by the tail. In fact, he was grasping it so hard that when he arced out of the cage, he pulled her over the top with him. They both sprawled on the lush, shag carpet.

For the first time in her life, Amber was free, and for a moment, all of her fears were forgotten. She gazed around. The room was a wonderland for a mouse. Ben's shoes, shirt, and pants lay by the lizard's cage. They were spread along the floor, like a fallen giant. There was all kinds of interesting junk in the room—dragon posters on the walls, a GameBoy, karate trophies on his dresser.

Ben seemed to have caught her mood. He stared up at the ceiling. "It's as big as a basketball arena," he whispered in awe.

Then he whined and clutched his chest. "I . . . my heart must be beating four hundred times a minute. I'm having a heart attack!"

"That's just normal," Amber said.

There was a scraping noise on the glass wall of the cage. Amber peered toward it. Imhotep was up on his back feet, his front claws gouging the glass as he tried to climb out. "Come back," he called. "I will not eat anyone. It was just a little joke, my American friends! A *tasteless* joke."

Ben crouched on his back feet, gasping for breath and swaying. "Okay," he told Amber. "Turn me back into a human."

Amber peered at him, unblinking. He was trying to stand. But he hadn't taken into account the changes that had occurred. He couldn't do much more than crouch. He wiggled the toes on his huge feet. Amber's whiskers twitched, and she sniffed a little. "I don't know how."

"But you're a wizard, right?" Ben demanded.

"No," Amber said. "I guess, maybe. I mean, uh, I don't know."

"Okay," Ben said, trying to sound calm and reasonable, and failing miserably. "Just *wish* me human again."

Amber squeaked angrily. "Why? Why should I do anything for you? One minute you're petting me like I'm your best friend and the next, I'm lizard bait."

"It wasn't my fault! Dad told me to!"

"Do you always feed your friends to lizards when your dad tells you?"

"It's not my fault, you little bean-sized rat," Ben growled. "Now, you made me into a mouse, and you're going to make me human again!" Ben balled his paws into fists and stalked toward Amber.

Amber had taken all she could from him. "You . . . stinkbug," she screamed. She leaped on him, knocking him backward to the floor. "You tried to kill me! You maggoty cousin of a mealworm!" She yanked out one of Ben's perfect whiskers.

"Ow," Ben cried.

Amber climbed on Ben and began pulling his ears, trying to rip them off. She was beside herself with rage. She bit Ben's nose.

"Knock it off," Ben yelled. He gave Amber a karate kick to the belly. It sent her hurtling backward five inches into the air, then tumbling over the rug. Amber landed with a thud. He'd kicked her so hard that tears sprang up in her eyes. She trembled badly.

"You fight like a sissy," Ben scolded.

"I fight like a mouse. There's a difference."

"Wish me back into a human," Ben shouted.

But she wanted to punish him. Besides, she wasn't sure she could even do it. Old Barley Beard had always insisted that she had magical powers. But as she looked at Ben, she didn't feel powerful. In fact, she was terrified. She was still shaking in fear of the lizard.

And if I turn him back into a human, she realized, *I'll be all alone*.

"I'm glad you're a mouse," she said angrily. "And if I have my way, you'll stay one forever."

Ben looked into her eyes and must have sensed her anger, for suddenly he backed away in terror.

* * *

Now, it is a strange fact that casting a spell gives off energy, just as lightning gives off electricity or a bonfire gives off heat. But when a spell goes off, it sends out a wave of magical energy—a cloud of plasma that only very powerful magicians can sense.

So when Amber turned Ben into a mouse, she released a magical force that exploded like a nuclear bomb.

In a swamp in Louisiana, an old bullfrog named Rufus Flycatcher was sitting atop a cypress knee at the edge of a bayou, croaking a long, complex spell that only a hearty old frog could master.

Waves of dark water lapped against the trees. A small gator was swimming through the bayou, eyeing Rufus, but Rufus didn't pay no never-mind. The ornery gator knew better than to try to gobble a wizard. Besides, there were a million frogs in the bayou tonight—all of them croaking up a storm.

Just below Rufus, five young frogs, practically tadpoles, listened patiently to Rufus's spell, a spell that would cause snapping turtles and loggerheads to flee the area, looking for prey other than young frogs to hunt. The spell was just beginning to take effect, spreading a luminous haze in the air above the swamp.

In the midst of this demonstration, Rufus felt the shock from Amber's spell, a force that shook him to his core. He whirled and saw the aura rising like a mushroom cloud.

"Urp!" Rufus gulped in amazement. The luminous haze overhead faded out.

One young frog at Rufus's knee, who was so much a tadpole that he hadn't even lost his tail yet, croaked, "What was that, Magi Flycatcher?"

"That," said Rufus, "was a powerful spell." He dared not guess what kind of spell had been cast, but he got a sinking feeling in his gut, an odd rumble, as if he'd eaten a big old wolf spider that just wouldn't stop wiggling. "Been more than a coon's age since I've seen an aura like that. A powerful mage is out there, for sure!"

"A light mage or dark?" the tadpole asked.

Rufus bit his lower lip in worry. The mage-storm had come from the far west, he felt sure. Dark sorcerers ruled the west. And the last time that Rufus had seen power unleashed like that, it heralded the coming of a great war where many good wizards had lost their lives.

We'll have to send a wizard to investigate, Rufus realized, and immediately he was lost in thought, wondering who might be able to make the journey at this time of year.

"We can only hope for good," Rufus croaked.

* * *

At the same time, in a cave near the coast, sixty miles from Ben's house, a sorcerer was half asleep, hanging from a rock by his feet, his wings draped dramatically about his body to keep it warm. His name was Nightwing. He had a silver ring in his nose, tarnished by age, and silver studs running around the edges of enormous ears that dwarfed his small face. His fur was the lovely color of orange coals among a dying fire, and bare patches along his wings and ears were tattooed with mystic symbols.

His heavy purple eyelids were closed as he chanted in a dream:

Once upon a midnight dreary,
While I pondered, weak and weary,
Over many a quaint and curious
Volume of forgotten lore,
While I nodded, nearly napping,
Suddenly there came a tapping—
As of someone gently rapping,
Rapping at my chamber door.

As the shock from Amber's spell rattled through the cave, Nightwing startled awake.

His mind was groggy from his long winter's hibernation, but he had seldom felt such immense power. Indeed, he had felt it only once, long ago, when the Cruel One first woke to his powers and began his reign of terror upon the earth. Nightwing opened his eyes.

All around him in the cave, his minions lay in torpor, deeply asleep. They were monstrous creatures, twisted things from nightmares. Only one of them sensed that something was amiss.

"What's that?" Nightwing's familiar, a tick that nestled near one ear, cried as plasma from the spell surged through the cave. In order to speak, the tick had to draw his proboscis painfully from Nightwing's flesh.

"'Tis a motley drama that has begun," Nightwing said, lifting his ears, "with much of Madness, and more of Sin, and Horror the soul of the plot."

"How *Poe*-etic," the tick, Darwin, said. "Does that mean I'll get some fresh blood to drink? You know, you're pretty much all tapped out."

Nightwing scrunched his nose in disgust. He wanted to eat the pest, and since Nightwing was an insectivore (despite persistent rumors that he was related to the great Count Dracula himself on his mother's side), he felt tempted to gobble Darwin down. But Nightwing needed the magic power that his familiar provided just as much as Darwin needed Nightwing's blood.

"Ah," Nightwing said, dropping from his perch as he took wing, heading toward the source of the power. "There will be blood for you, my lovely. There will be blood."

It does kind of look like a snake, *he thought groggily.*

CHAPTER 9

A MOTHER'S LOVE

No love is so certain and pure as a mother's love!
—Barley Beard

Ben turned away from Amber in fear, sprang under his bedroom door, and waddled toward the stairs. In his short life, there had always been one certainty: though his mother lacked common sense and good personal hygiene, she'd always loved him. She'd always been there to bandage his boo-boos.

His stubby legs couldn't carry him down to his mom fast enough. Nothing on his body moved right. He felt like he was wearing clown shoes. It took all of his concentration just to walk, and every few paces he had to leap thirty feet down to the next stair step. His tail thumped each time he landed, until finally he whirled and yelled at it, "Quit following me. You give me the creeps!"

Ben wheezed. He was amazed at the smells on the carpet. His powerful mouse nose picked up the strong odors of spilled grape juice and a crumb from a peanut butter sandwich he'd sneaked to his room last month.

Amber raced nimbly beside him, hopping on her back legs and landing on her front paws. "What are you doing? Where are you going? You won't leave me, will you?" She sounded frightened. "I've never been out of my cage before."

Ben ignored her. He felt glad that she was scared. It served her right!

He stumbled past the Christmas tree, still petrifying in the corner, and limped beneath wads of wrapping paper as large as buses.

By the time he reached the kitchen, a hike of at least a mile, he felt as if he'd collapse. His heart raced hundreds of beats a minute, and his mouth had begun to foam.

He passed a line of black ants marching across the kitchen floor. As they marched, they sang:

All us bugs up in the cupboard,
Love to work the whole night long.
We aren't lazy; we aren't crazy.
We are bold and cruel and strong.
Just as butterflies like sunshine,
Just as slugs love driving rain,
Us bugs love to sing and dance—
Kick your mama in the pants!—
Us bugs love to sing and dance
Around the kitchen drain!

Ben watched the ants caper, feeling as if he'd just taken a wrong turn into the Twilight Zone.

He scampered onto the kitchen floor and found his feet sliding on the linoleum with each step. It was almost like being in an ice-skating rink. He passed the fridge and saw a dark alley between it and the wall. Dust bunnies the size of tumbleweeds lurked in the corners.

A cockroach careened giddily across the kitchen floor like a remote control car that's gone berserk, barreled into Ben, and shouted, "Everyone to the pantry! Someone left the Cap'n Crunch open, and we're having a luau!"

Ben stared at the cockroach, dumbfounded.

Then he ducked under the kitchen counter and peered up at his mother. There she towered, bigger than the Statue of Liberty. She was staring mournfully from a mountain of moldy dishes to the ceiling and mumbling under her breath, "Please, bless me with a maid . . . "

"Mom!" Ben squeaked. "Down here. Help!"

But with the rumble of the TV in the other room—Dad was watching *Pokémon*—she couldn't hear him.

Ben studied her pant leg. She wore khaki Dockers. He wondered if he could hook his little claws into the fabric and scurry up like a cat.

He leaped clumsily into the air, rising at least sixty feet, grabbed her knee, and started to climb. With only four fingers on each front paw, it was a truly heroic task.

The results were astonishing.

His mom must have felt something on her knee. She glanced down and screamed.

She fell backward, knocking over the moldy dishes, then leaped about five feet and kicked with all her might. Ben hurtled through the air, slammed into the refrigerator, slid down, and thudded to the floor. Dishes crashed, like flying saucers shot out of the sky, and shattered on the linoleum. Huge chunks of crockery skidded everywhere, and Ben leaped out of the way as a jagged piece slid under him.

"Help," his mom screamed. "A mouse!"

Ben struggled to his feet, dodged as a shattered cup went rolling past. "Mom," he squeaked. "It's me!" He limped toward her and squatted on the floor, peering up. White foam dribbled from his mouth, and he wiped it off with the back of one paw.

"Help," she screamed louder. "A *rabid* mouse!"

"Mom," Ben said, "it's me!"

Amber scurried to the fridge just behind Ben's back and hid under the door.

Ben's dad bounded into the kitchen and grabbed a spatula from the stove. "I'll bet it's that mouse Ben is supposed to feed the lizard."

"No," Mom shouted in a panic. "There are two of them!"

Ben's dad peered down at him. His eyes grew fearful.

He studied Ben with growing alarm. "You're right. It *is* a rabid mouse! Call 911 while I hold him off." He raised the spatula protectively.

His mom rushed out to the living room.

"Dad," Ben called. "It's just me!"

"Honey," Ben's dad shouted, "it's squeaking really *strangely*."

"It's no use," Amber called to Ben. "You're a mouse now. Humans can't understand us—just like we can't understand them."

Ben's mind did a little flip. "What do you mean, you can't understand humans?" Ben asked Amber. "I understand them just fine."

"Maybe that's because you were human once."

Ben's dad crouched. Suddenly, it seemed that he had heard enough of Ben's odd squeaking. His dad cocked his arm and swung.

Ben tried to leap away, but he was too slow. His dad whacked him with the spatula. Ben slammed into the floor. Stars whirled in his vision. He tried to climb to his feet, but he was too weak and too sick to his stomach.

His mom thundered back into the kitchen. The floor shook as if a herd of rhinos were charging.

"Did you call the cops?" Dad asked.

"No," she said, "I got a better idea."

Ben heard the electric whine of a motor.

From under the fridge, Amber shouted in terror, "Snake! She's got a snake!"

Ben peered up weakly. He saw a huge gaping tunnel with a silver rim. A powerful wind raced around him. He realized that he was staring straight up into the nozzle of the vacuum cleaner!

It does kind of look like a snake, he thought groggily.

"Ben," Amber yelled. "Run this way!" From the corner of his eye, Ben spotted Amber lunging around the corner into the living room. In desperation, he hurried after her, kicking with both rear feet, trying to land on his hands the way that Amber did.

He careened into the living room and peered around. The big-screen TV squatted amid walls of garish lava lamps, each a different size and color. Overhead hovered his mom's mirror ball. On really bad days, she'd ingest half a cup of sugar and just sit in the easy chair, watching the mirror ball whirl in circles as she listened to her *My Turn on Earth* CD.

Ben spotted Amber climbing up the brass chains of his mom's cuckoo clock.

"Up here," Amber shouted as she neared the top. "I see a dark hole!"

Ben trundled to the clock, leaped as high as he could, and caught the chains. Kicking and clawing, he boosted himself up the chain by sheer willpower until he collapsed safely inside the hole.

For a moment, he lay next to Amber, his heart pounding. He could smell the powerful odors of lacquer, glue, and wood. The clock was the size of his bedroom, except that huge gears with notched teeth lined every wall. Afraid that a gear would catch his tail, he climbed higher and perched on a slab next to the carved figure of a little cuckoo bird with blue wings, a white head, and yellow beak.

Ben's mother called, "Where did they go? Look under the couch." The vacuum cleaner whirred louder as it drew close.

"Honey," Ben's dad said, half in astonishment and half as a compliment. "When did you learn to use a vacuum cleaner?"

"Last month," she said with great pride. "I took a night class at the university."

They began rustling around in the living room.

"Where are we?" Amber whispered to Ben. "Are they trying to eat us? Does this always happen when you get out of your cage?"

"Quiet!" Ben hissed. "They'll hear us."

"Ben?" his dad shouted. "Ben, where are you?"

For half a second, Ben wondered if his dad had somehow recognized his voice or maybe realized that Ben had turned into a mouse.

Maybe he'll even know how to fix me, Ben thought.

He began to squeak a reply, when his dad added, "Come down here and help us catch these mice!"

Ben's heart sank. A clicking noise startled Ben, and the clock began to chime.

Gong!

The slab beneath Ben slid forward, and a little pair of wooden doors flung open. Cuckoo! the clock sounded from a whistle behind Ben's head.

Ben's parents turned to stare. His father was moving the piano so that his mom could look under it. But now they gaped as Ben quivered on the wooden perch, a hundred yards above the floor.

The plank slid back, and the doors closed.

"Let's get out of here," Ben shrieked.

Amber began to race down the chain, head first, but Ben doubted that he could manage such a feat.

Gong! went the clock again. The plank slid forward.

Suddenly Ben was out in space, like a swimmer on a high-dive board, only he didn't have any water to jump into and all of the spectators wanted him dead.

Cuckoo! sounded the clock.

Mom headed for Ben, vacuum cleaner aimed like a cannon.

Ben tried to tell his legs to jump, but they went as limp as yarn.

In seconds, the wind grabbed him and sucked him down. He clung to the lip of the vacuum and hung on for dear life.

"Mom, help," he cried.

But his mother said, "Oh, no you don't," reached down, and pried his fingers loose.

The vacuum slurped him through a long tunnel, as if he were on a waterslide. His chin slammed painfully against the ribs of the vacuum hose.

"Heeeeelp!" he screamed.

Then he thudded into a dark chamber amid a pile of dust, lint, hair, and dead bugs. Through the plastic housing of the vacuum, he could see distorted images of his mom and dad as they chased Amber. The vacuum's motor whined deafeningly, and dust swirled. It lodged in his fur, wedged into his lips, stung his eyes, clogged his ears and nostrils.

Ben gasped. There was too much dust in the air. Every time he drew a breath, he felt as if he'd cough his lungs out. He covered his snout with his little paws and hunched over, struggling to breathe.

After painful seconds, he fainted and fell. It seemed that he was falling, falling, for several long minutes. Then everything went black.

"Wild mice," Amber wondered. Would they be friendly?

CHAPTER 5

STRANGE CRITTERS

Everyone likes a mole in his hole,
And mice can be nice too.
But remember, my child, wherever you go,
NEVER trust a shrew!

—A COMMON RHYME TAUGHT AMONG VOLES

AMBER SLOWLY WOKE FROM a nightmare in which an enormous metal python was swallowing her. Her chin thunked against its ribs as she slid down. Yet as she woke, the reality was as bad as the dream. She heard Ben's dad grumbling as humans do, but she couldn't understand him.

"Here kitty, kitty, kitty," Ben's dad called. "Come get the mice. Tasty little mice for a nice kitty."

Amber tumbled in a cloud of dust, over and over, until she landed with a thud on something hard. She began to cough the grit from her lungs.

Dimly, she recalled how the humans had cornered her and sucked her into the vacuum cleaner.

"Amber, are you all right?" Ben called weakly.

She shivered. The night was cold and wet, as is common in Oregon during winter.

"Where are we?" Amber asked. Her eyes were full of dust. They stung too much for her to want to open them. She sniffed. She could smell lush grass and ice and foggy night air. In all of her dreams, she'd never imagined such scents. "It smells . . . glorious!" She raised her snout high. "Is this . . . the Endless Meadow?"

"This," Ben said dryly, "is a garbage can."

She cracked open her eyes. She lay in a huge container. Now she could smell more than grass and night air. She tasted a riot of odors. Old washrags in the garbage can vied with rotting food and paint thinner to see which could give off the most noxious fumes.

Despite the fact that only the stars and a moon behind a cloud gave any light, Amber could see well. She lay sprawled in an old sardine tin, with wads of newspaper, crumpled cereal boxes, and smelly cans all around. A crusty sardine had cushioned her fall. Amber peered up. Ben loomed over her, a shadow against the starlight.

"Let's find a place to hide," Ben urged, "before the neighbor's cat, Domino, comes."

Alarms went off in Amber's mind. She'd seen an evil kitten at the pet shop—spike toothed with fiery green eyes that glowed with cruelty. It had purred threats as a customer carried it around.

Amber leaped to her feet.

Ben tottered away from her through the garbage, slogging amidst a quagmire of baked beans, climbing a can that rolled crazily beneath his feet, then tiptoeing along a newspaper until he could peer down.

"You know, it can't be more than three feet to the ground, but it looks like I'm peering over a cliff."

"What's that?" Amber asked. She pointed to a wall of boards with white pickets aimed at the moon, sealing off the neighbor's yard. "Are we in a big cage?"

"It's a fence," Ben said. "I guess it *is* a cage, sort of. People build them around their houses."

"Humans live in their own cages?" Amber asked.

From the corner of her eye, Amber saw something huge and monstrous suddenly move to the side. She let out a startled yelp. "What's that?" The Something swayed like a giant above the houses.

"Just a pine tree."

"Oh." Amber had never heard of a tree before. "Do they eat mice?"

"Nah, it's a plant—like grass or moss, only bigger."

"Then why is it moving?" Amber demanded.

"The wind is blowing it."

"Wind?" Amber asked. "What's wind? Is it bigger than a tree?" She imagined some hideous monster knocking trees aside in its effort to eat her.

"Don't be stupid," Ben said.

Amber cried, "Why didn't anyone ever warn me about these things?" Tears welled up in her eyes. She felt alone in a strange and terrifying world. *No*, she realized, *I'm not alone. I'm worse than alone, because I'm with Ben.* "And I'm not stupid," she said angrily. "I just don't know anything."

Amber heard a cat meow behind the fence.

"Come on," Ben whispered. He clung to the lip of the garbage can with his rear feet and stretched his nose toward the ground, searching for something to hang onto as he lowered himself. He used his tail to balance for a moment, but suddenly fell.

He hit the ground. "Now you."

Amber leaped from the garbage can. Stalks of grass took her weight, and then sprang her back up. She'd hardly felt the ground at all. "Fun!"

"Quiet!" Ben said, slapping a paw over Amber's mouth.

He peered up at the picket fence. A black, shadowy form suddenly appeared atop it. Amber could make out a wiry tail and two pyramids for ears. It was Domino!

The cat perched atop the fence, its tail waving in excited jerks. It sniffed the air and, for a long moment, just peered toward the trash can.

"Don't move," Ben whispered. He pulled Amber down, so that they could both hide in the deep grass.

The cat crouched and wiggled its rump as it set its feet. Its ears drew back, and it went as still as could be, trying to make itself invisible.

Amber didn't dare move.

For long minutes, the cat crouched, waiting. The grass that the mice hid in smelled overpowering, and the damp ground gave off hundreds of strange and subtle scents.

Ben reached down and picked some grass, deftly twisted it, and put it on his head. He smeared mud on his face.

Atop the fence, Domino purred a little song:

Nibble, nibble, on the mice,
With their heads off, they look nice!
Though they're fast, I'll run much faster,
    And drag their corpse
    To the porch,
As a present for my master!

Just then, a yowl came from the street. A tomcat shouted, "Hey, Domino, what you doing?"

"Hunting mice," Domino hissed, leaping from the fence into the neighbor's yard. Amber heard the two cats softly making plans. Domino hissed, "You run around the front and flush them into the backyard. I'll do the lion thing and snag them as they run past."

"Yeah, yeah," the second cat hissed.

"Come on," Ben whispered. He and Amber scampered through the tall dry grass into the backyard, scuttling beneath a forest of weeds before the cats had time to carry out their plan. They stopped to catch their breath, and Ben pointed to the woven grass on his hair.

"You want some?"

"I may not know much," Amber said, "but that doesn't mean that I want to *look* stupid."

"It's not stupid. It's camouflage. To the cats, we'll just look like a pile of grass."

"Aren't there animals that eat grass?"

"Yeah," Ben said. "Cows and horses and stuff."

"So what difference does it make if you get eaten by something that eats mice or something that eats grass?"

Ben thought for a long moment, then with some embarrassment, he pulled the twisted grass from his head.

He led the way through a field of dandelions under the dark pine that leaned overhead, keeping themselves deep in the shadows. Huge pinecones the size of buses laid scattered atop beds of moldy pine needles. Unearthly mushrooms grew in little groves of white and yellow. A giant slug oozed across the ground like a booger that had come to life.

Amber heard strange noises, the groaning of wood, the hissing of leaves in the wind, the cries of night birds. Some startled creature went thumping away. Everywhere she looked, odd leaves, shaped like snouts, waggled in the shadows under the breeze.

"Where are we going?" Amber asked.

"Underground," Ben said. "I know a place where there are some wild mice. I caught Domino trying to eat one here last summer."

"Wild mice," Amber wondered. Would they be friendly? Or would they bite her tail?

Finally, the woods opened, and they reached a dark tree. Ben poked his nose in the pine needles at its base.

"What are you looking for?" Amber asked.

"Ah, found it!" Ben peered down a black hole, like an open mouth, leading under the pine needles.

Amber crept close and sniffed. She could smell a bitter scent at the mouth of the tunnel—urine. "No *mice* live here," Amber said, warily. "It smells strange."

"Sure they do," Ben said.

Ben squeezed into the hole and began crawling on all fours. Amber couldn't see a thing, but her whiskers were just the right length to brush against the sides of the burrow as she crawled. Amber trailed so close to Ben that she kept stepping on his tail.

The burrow slanted down and down, veered, then circled back up. It was almost like being inside the vacuum hose. Amber felt strange, frightening things brushing against her ears. The passage broadened. They crept past a black opening that smelled of poop, but kept to the main tunnel.

"I sure wish I had some light," Ben said.

"Me too," Amber added.

Suddenly a pebble in front of them began to glow. At first it was only a soft light, almost as if Amber imagined it, but then the pebble went as clear as the glass on her old cage, and a brilliant light poured from it, chasing the shadows through the hole ahead.

"You *are* a wizard," Ben said in amazement. He turned back and peered at her. She felt as surprised as he.

Ben reached down with one paw. He touched the pebble experimentally. He picked it up, revealing the way ahead.

The walls of the burrow were worn smooth, but white things dangled down like limp whiskers.

"What are those white things?" Amber asked.

"Roots from the tree," Ben whispered. He heard a moaning sound and saw something pinkish that oozed backward into a small hole. "And that's a worm."

Amber heard a scuffling ahead. She looked forward, where the burrow twisted away, and saw a pair of bright eyes peering at them—cruel eyes.

"Who's there?" an old critter called gruffly. He sounded angry. Very angry.

He had a grizzled face, bright black eyes, and long whiskers, much like Amber's.

"Just a couple of lost mice," Ben answered, "searching for a place to stay the night."

"Keep right there until I can sniff you," the old critter said.

Amber heard the small pad of the fellow's feet as he squeezed through the burrow. He was a fat mouse, Amber decided. He sniffed at Ben, and Amber caught a wild scent—clean fur and meadows.

"Phew," the creature said. "Dirty mice! Mice in our burrow. Well, we're gentlefolk. Besides, it wasn't always *our* burrow. Mice dug it in the first place. My name's Vervane. Come along."

Vervane spun with a bit of a grunt—a real trick in the narrow tunnel—then padded away.

Amber could smell him better now and felt sure that Vervane wasn't a mouse after all. Besides, his tail was way too short.

They moved swiftly to a large chamber where fungi clung to the pine roots that dangled from the roof. Ben's light showed that nice dry leaves, grass stalks, and hair littered the floor. The old critter looked grizzled. Fur covered most of his ears.

A dozen of his kin nestled in the corners of the chamber, including a mother who lay on her side, nursing some young kittens. All of the strange critters were like Vervane—nasty and grizzled, with short, unsightly tails.

One young girl shouted, "Grandpa, Grandpa, who's here?"

"Mice," Vervane said with disdain. "A dirty pair of them. Queer folk, carrying a star."

"Mice?" the girl asked. Her small dark eyes grew wide, and she gazed at Amber and Ben with a mixture of wonder and suspicion. She bounded forward and gaped in awe at the light that Ben held. "Hi. My name is Meadowsweet. Is it true that you eat grubs?"

"Of course not—" Ben started to say.

But Amber burst in, "I've never eaten a bug myself, but I hear that they can be quite tasty."

Ben looked at Amber, his jaw dropping in surprise. The human boy apparently didn't understand much about mice at all.

"Aren't you mice?" Ben asked the folks in the burrow, for they *looked* very mouselike.

"Of course not," Meadowsweet said. "We're the peaceful folk of the meadows and woods—the voles. We only eat plants, not flesh."

Meadowsweet ran around Ben and Amber in a circle, and three others her size joined in. They began to sing:

In grain fields in summer, among berries and
vines,
The peaceful folk of the field you will find,
Cutting down wheat stalks, gathering oats,
Picking up pine nuts and preening their coats.
Then they carry their food, down to their holes.
They are the voles, peace-loving voles.

The girls ended the song by dropping to their backs and wriggling their paws in the air as they giggled.

Amber smiled. Every moment since Ben had brought her to his home had been terrifying. But for the first time all night, she felt safe.

"Come on," the young ones shouted.

"You have a song, don't you?"

"Sing us your song!"

Ben shrugged and hung his head, too embarrassed to sing. "I don't have one."

"Don't you at least have a song to tell us what you are?" old Vervane demanded.

"I . . . I don't need a song," Ben said. "I'm a human!"

The voles gaped in astonishment. The glowing stone alone was miraculous, but this was too much.

Vervane's mouth dropped. "Say again?"

"I'm human," Ben affirmed.

The mother vole whispered to Vervane, "Maybe he got kicked in the head by a bullfrog or something . . ."

"It's true," Amber said. "He is human, or *was*, until just awhile ago. Then something happened, and he turned into a mouse."

Old Vervane eyed them suspiciously, as if he didn't much like mice and trusted them even less. "What happened, exactly?"

Ben pointed at Amber with one finger of his paw. "It's her fault. She turned me into a mouse." Tears of rage formed in his eyes, and Ben began shaking, as if eager to be able to tell on Amber.

The voles drew back in fear, eyes growing wide, as their suspicion turned to Amber.

"Is this so?" The old vole's eyes narrowed.

Amber nodded slightly.

"Are you a good wizardess," Vervane asked in a kindly tone, then sneered, "or a naughty one?"

"I . . . I don't know," Amber said, feeling deep inside her, looking for an answer. "I've never done magic before. It just sort of happened."

"I don't know much," Vervane said, his voice dripping with accusation, "But I've been around for a couple of years, and I can tell you this: transmogrification spells don't just happen. That's high enchantment!"

The mother vole offered, "She's young. She doesn't look like a dark mage. She's just a scared little mouse."

"That's the problem," Vervane groused. "She's a mouse. A vicious, bug-gobbling mouse. I don't trust 'em. Especially pocket mice! They look all big-eyed and innocent—right to the second that they snatch your young! I haven't seen a mouse around here in months, and I'm not happy about these ones."

"It's not as if she were a shrew," the mother said. "And she's not a pocket mouse or anything quite so dangerous. She's a . . . a *house* mouse."

"Yes," Vervane agreed, "a lazy vermin that lives off human scraps, gnawing through walls and stealing from the kitchen. I don't like their kind, and I don't want them here."

Amber felt astonished to learn she and her folk had such a foul reputation among voles. There was a tense, embarrassing silence, and old Vervane looked as if he might bite her, when suddenly a handsome young vole darted from the shadows and addressed Ben. "Wait a minute. So you're the one, aren't you?"

"The one?"

"The boy who lives in the house next to Domino? You're the boy who saved me last summer. Domino had me in her claws when you threw a pinecone and drove her away."

Ben gulped. He seemed to have forgotten about that. "Yeah, that was me," he said proudly.

"Thank you," the vole said, eyes shining with gratitude. "My name is Bushmaster. I'm forever in your debt."

Bushmaster turned to the younger voles and, in a voice choked with emotion, said, "These are my friends. Get them some food. They must be hungry."

The young voles went scampering through the burrow as Bushmaster led Ben and Amber to a cozy corner.

But Amber felt somehow betrayed. Why had Ben saved a strange vole but hadn't saved her? It didn't make any sense. She suspected that it wasn't that he liked her or hated her, it was just that she was beneath his notice. Perhaps the life of a mouse or a vole didn't mean much to him.

Soon the young voles reappeared carrying in their mouths loads of pine nuts, bits of blackberry jerky, dried flowers of jasmine, clover, and buttercup, and pieces of grass and mushrooms. They set the food on a dry leaf in front of Ben and Amber until they had a large pile heaped before them.

Ben pawed through the food, and Amber did too. For Amber, it was strange and exotic stuff after a lifetime of eating mouse pellets. Ben declared, "This is almost as good as the trail mix my mom buys at 7-11."

The voles all laughed.

Amber ignored the bulbs of alfalfa root but found that she liked the honeyed taste of clover and jasmine, along with the pine nuts and dried berries.

Soon she was full.

"A story," a young one called. "Tell us a story, Grandpa! Or better yet, sing us a song!"

Old Vervane stammered with embarrassment. "No, no. Not in front of our guests. Besides you've heard all of my stories and songs." He peered pointedly at Ben. "Perhaps you have a story or a song—something human?"

Ben thought a moment and smiled. "I know a song," he said. "A song about mice." He began singing softly. Amber recognized the tune from the pet shop, for Feeder had often hummed it when she brought the mouse pellets. But this was the first time that she understood the words. Ben sang:

Three blind mice, three blind mice.
See how they run, see how they run.
They all ran after the farmer's wife,
She cut off their tails with a carving knife,
Did you ever see such a sight in your life
As three blind mice? Three blind mice.

Amber felt shocked to the bone. It was a dismal tune about an agrarian's spouse who assaulted visually impaired rodents and performed acts of mayhem upon their tails!

As he sang, the voles began shivering, backing away in terror. But Ben never noticed. Instead, he sang lightly, as if it were a joke. The song was a cruel reminder that Ben wasn't really a mouse at all.

"Is that what humans do to mice?" she demanded when the song was done. Ben looked away guiltily. "I mean . . . back in the pet shop, I . . . we thought that you humans embraced mice.

We thought you took us home, fed us, and loved us. We thought that we meant something to you!"

The voles watched in silent shock.

"We don't chop off their tails. Honest!" Ben said. His whiskers twitched nervously.

Quick as the thought flashed through her mind, Amber remembered her mother and old Barley Beard and all of the rest of the pet shop mice that the humans had embraced. Where had they gone?

Amber began to shake from more than the frigid night air. She demanded, "Ben, what do you humans do with mice?"

Ben ducked, looked away. "I don't know."

"What happened to my mother, my family, my friends?" Amber pressed. She wanted to know, regardless of how much it hurt, so she wished that Ben would tell her the truth.

Ben began to shake and struggle and gasp for breath. He tried to turn away, but Amber's spell forced the words out of him. In a strangled voice he confessed, "I don't know for sure. But when I bought you, you were cheap. I thought it was just because you weren't as pretty as the spotted mice . . . But there was a sign on your cage, a sign that said 'Feeder Mice.' And now I know. You were raised to be food for snakes and lizards."

Amber let out a cry. Not just for her mother and family, but for all mice through all time that had been raised as feeder mice and born to the cage.

"All of them?" Amber said. "All of them are eaten? You humans don't love any of us? You *never* take us home?"

Ben said, "Mostly, we kill mice," Ben admitted. "We put out traps for them or poison." Then by way of apology, he added, "But sometimes we keep mice as pets."

"Just the colored mice," Amber realized. "The expensive ones in the fancy cages, the ones that get to play on exercise wheels and eat the tastiest foods."

Ben didn't deny it.

"I wanted to keep you," Ben said. "I wanted you for a friend." There was a long silence, during which Amber couldn't speak. A friend? How could they be friends?

Tears flowed freely from her eyes.

Her life as a free mouse had just begun, but she felt as if it were the end of the world.

"I have to go back," Amber said. "I have to go back to the pet shop and free them." She didn't know where to go. The world was such a strange and dangerous place.

Ben looked at her for a long time, shaking. "It's a long way to the pet shop, and the trip would be dangerous for a mouse."

"You had better come with me," Amber said. "If you don't, I'll . . . I'll turn you into a . . . a—"

"What? A slug?" Ben asked, as if nothing that she did to him could hurt him any more than she already had.

"No, I'll turn your whole family into mice." Deep inside, she felt a dark power rising.

Ben backed away in terror.

"All right," he said after a moment. "I'll take you to the pet shop and help you free the mice. But afterward, I want something from you in return. I want you to free me. You have to turn me back into a human."

Amber smiled. She was getting what she wanted—even if she did have to take it by force.

I really would make an excellent evil wizardess, she thought.

Nightwing dipped toward the source, circling.
His enormous ears picked up human voices in an upper chamber.

NIGHTWING

By the pricking of my thumbs,
Something wicked this way comes.
—WILLIAM SHAKESPEARE

IN THE CHILL AIR, Nightwing scrabbled across the sky. The stars rode through the heavens above, while dark forests seethed below. He could still sense Amber's spell. After-fires from it could be seen in the west, a glowing column of magical purple flame. As he flew, he sang:

Hear the tolling of the bells—
Iron bells!
What a world of solemn thought their monopoly compels!
In the silence of the night,
How we shiver with affright
At the melancholy menace of their tone!

"Quiet," Darwin screamed. "Not that poem again!" He buried his head deep in the flesh of Nightwing's armpit and tried to shut the sound out by wrapping all eight legs over his ears. "Do any poem but that one. My head is ringing. I can't take it anymore." He went from pleading to a more dangerous tone. "One more verse, and I swear by my mother's proboscis, I'll sever your jugular!"

"You palavering parasite," Nightwing said. "You can no more appreciate the genius of poetry than a sow can appreciate a Van Gogh. Edgar Allen Poe was the greatest human poet of all time. Compared with him, Dante Alighieri spouted drivel, and Shakespeare's verses are but the scribblings of a hack."

Nightwing fluttered toward a house, squeaking in his loudest voice,

And the people—ah, the people—
They that dwell up in the steeple,
All alone,

Darwin gouged his proboscis into Nightwing's side and threatened, "I smell a gizzard!"

"Look," Nightwing shouted. "The source of the spells, spells, spells! Keeping time, time, time, in a sort of runic rhyme!"

He wheeled gleefully above a house in a dark neighborhood at the edge of a town. The streetlight below glowed forlornly, and only a few cars crawled upon the road. But the light from magic spells sputtered below with an eerie purple gleam, pulsing on and off like a candle that gutters from lack of air as it suffocates.

Nightwing dropped low, searching for any animals that had a magical aura. A pair of cats hunted behind the house, but they were nothing special. In front of the house, a police car was parked, its lights flashing blue and white.

The residue of the magical spell was centered *within* the house.

Nightwing dipped toward the source, circling. His enormous ears picked up human voices in an upper chamber. "We came up here and found his clothes draped across the floor," Ben's dad said. "But Ben was just . . . gone."

"It's like he popped," his mom added. "Like he was a big balloon, and he just popped, and all of his clothes dropped to the floor."

The police officer said in a bored tone, "Well, if he'd popped, his skin would be here too. I think he just ran off."

"But," his mom asked, "where would he go without his clothes?"

"Skinny-dipping?" the cop suggested.

Nightwing dived toward the roof. He was an instant from death when he cast a tiny spell. As he hit the wooden shingles, the roof shattered.

He found himself in a room where bright lights blinded him. He dropped to the floor.

With a thought, he dimmed the lights to a softer hue. The humans stood gaping at him, looking back and forth between him and the hole in the roof.

"A bat," Ben's mother screamed frantically. "Shoot it!"

The police officer stood in shock, staring at Nightwing as Ben's mom grabbed for his gun. She fumbled with the holster strap for half a second until the officer realized what she was doing and tried to knock her hand away.

Nightwing glared at the humans. He was a wise bat, capable of understanding human speech, for he had spent long decades in its study. So in a loud voice, a voice of hissing and thunder that shook the ceiling and made paint flake from the walls, he commanded, "Leave us—unless you want me to stuff you into the microwave and pop you like corn!"

Ben's mom screamed, babbling, "It talked to us. That bat talked to us." Her husband staggered back as if he'd been slapped.

"Vampire," the cop muttered, trembling in fear. He drew his revolver and tried to steady his hand to take aim.

With a thought, Nightwing magically knocked the gun from his hand. It went bouncing on the floor and discharged. The bullet slammed into a Pooh bear, and fluff exploded all through the room. Nightwing smiled evilly at the bear and cast a small spell. Blood began gushing from its wound, and it cried in a horrified voice, "Help! He'll kill us all!"

The humans stood staring in shock, so Nightwing growled, "If you don't get out of here, I'll see to it that you spend an eternity in charge of stacking the folding chairs for my master's weekly rallies—in H-e-double-toothpicks!"

The humans fled, stumbling over and clawing each other in their hurry. The cop shoved the others aside and went out first, tripping and tumbling downstairs, then Ben's mom and dad rushed through the door.

Nightwing sent a thought that slammed the door tight. Suddenly, roots grew out of the wooden door panels and burrowed deep into the walls, fusing the walls and doors together.

"That ought to hold them for awhile," Darwin said.

The magical glow came from the lizard's terrarium. Nightwing turned his attention to Imhotep. The Nile monitor stood regally in his cage, just beneath his sun lamp, eyeing Nightwing stalwartly.

He'll pay for his pride, Nightwing thought, studying the lizard's fine skin.

But he took a soft tone with the lizard. "A powerful wizard cast a spell here not more than an hour ago. Tell me about it."

Imhotep had no choice in the matter. He told about Ben and Amber. And when the lizard finished, Nightwing drew close to the lizard's cage and whispered, "You have a cruel heart, lizard. I think it should never beat again."

Imhotep looked fearfully at the bat, then gasped, and sank to the floor of the cage, dead from a heart attack.

Now that Nightwing was sure that the lizard would never speak again, he flew up through the hole in the roof.

"So a mouse who has never cast a spell performed a transmogrification on a human," he mused. "That's a spell that most sorcerers wouldn't dare attempt after a lifetime of study . . . This girl has talent."

"She sounds dangerous," Darwin said. "What are you going to do about her?"

That question weighed heavily on Nightwing's mind as he circled the house. By now, the police officer was in his car, frantically calling for backup in order to handle the vampire. As soon as he noticed Nightwing, he ran to his trunk and pulled out a shotgun. Nightwing was tempted to teach the mortal a lesson, but he didn't want the man's dying screams to alert Amber and Ben.

Darwin urged, "As you've often said, only the strongest can be permitted to survive."

Nightwing shot back, "And you're the one who is always saying, 'Just because you want to take over the world, you don't have to be so mean about it.'"

"I was just hoping . . ." Darwin began.

"What?"

"For a little bloodshed."

Nightwing snickered. "In good time." He was a powerful sorcerer, the greatest in the west. But he had been hiding now for decades, since the Great War, slowly regrowing his power. He didn't dare let this young wizardess stay alive, lest she interfere with his plans.

So he winged back up into the top of the big pine behind the house. He could *feel* Amber's power. He didn't know what rock she was hiding under, but he knew that she was near.

He took a position in one of the lower boughs.

"What are we doing here?" Darwin asked.

Nightwing cast a magic spell to boost his sensitive hearing and perked up his ears. He had to move them back and forth a bit in order to avoid picking up radio signals from the local radio station. "Quiet," Nightwing said, scrunching forward. "I hear mice . . ."

* * *

Back in the burrow, Ben's confession had had a chilling effect on the voles. For a bit, they seemed distant and quiet, and Ben sulked in embarrassment at being forced to admit what humans did to mice.

Indeed, the voles all fell silent until young Bushmaster shouted, "Hey, let's have some fun." He began to sing:

When your fur gets all dirty,
Let it be your cue—
Don't stink up your burrow;
Go run through the dew!

When the morning grass is wet,
You can sure have fun
Scrubbing off your belly
If you do it on the run!

Go and leave your odor—
Don't let it follow you!
Find yourself a meadow
And run through the dew!

The song was obviously a favorite with the younger voles, who capered about, hopping madly as if forging through the grass in order to bathe in the morning dew.

From then on, the voles seemed to almost forget Ben. All night long they told stories and sang and danced around Amber's light. It was a joyous celebration, unlike anything that Ben had ever witnessed. The voles played games, chasing each other's tails, and when they tired, they feasted again, and the whole party started over.

Ben had a merry time but soon began feeling drowsy. Lest he fall asleep without his nightly prayer, he found a quiet corner and prayed softly but fervently, "Thank You for all of my blessings." He had to stop to think of things that he was thankful for. "Thank You for this burrow, with its roots and warm leaves. Thank You for the . . . the trail mix of . . . ugh . . . dried fungi, even if it did smell questionable and have lots of vole spit on it."

Now that he felt he had expressed appropriate thanks, he felt free to beg. Sniffling, he pleaded, "Please, please, I really *hate* being a mouse. If this was supposed to teach me something—like you shouldn't feed your friends to lizards—then I've learned my lesson. So will You please, please turn me back?"

He sat for a moment hoping that God would answer, but nothing happened. No burning bush, no angel. Not even a strong hunch as to what to do.

What if I can never turn back into a human? Ben wondered. Would it be so bad to live here, in the backyard, under a pine tree with some friendly voles? He'd still be close to his mom and dad, he imagined, and that might make him feel sort of safe when he went to sleep—even though he wouldn't have his football helmet on or a baseball bat hidden with him under the covers.

But now Ben could hear the voles whispering to Amber, holding a council. Vervane and Bushmaster warned of nearby dangers. There were local cats and dogs, which Ben had known about, but there were other predators too—like a crotchety old opossum, crows, an owl, a pair of grey foxes that came down from the hills in winter, a mink that sometimes wandered from the mill pond, pine snakes that slithered into burrows and ate whole families, and even a tarantula that hid under Ben's own house.

If Ben had known of all these carnivores, he'd have been afraid to cross his own backyard.

I've got to find a weapon in the morning, Ben thought.

With that, he lay with his eyes closed, as if asleep, lulled by tales of narrow escape that Vervane spun with the expertness of an orb spider.

* * *

Nightwing smiled and chuckled evilly.

"What did they say?" Darwin shouted, leaping up and down with excitement.

"There's trouble in paradise," Nightwing snickered. "And I didn't even have to stir it up myself. The boy doesn't like being a mouse, it seems."

Nightwing glanced down at the tick and considered. "Darwin, what do you do when someone hands you a lemon?"

The tick thought, then answered, "Run like the wind before it squishes me?"

"No, you gluttonous little gob sucker," Nightwing said. "You smash the lemon against his face and rub his snout in it until it turns to lemonade."

"Oh, I get it," the tick said, completely baffled.

"Quiet," Nightwing hissed. "They're speaking again . . ."

* * *

"So you intend to go through with it?" Vervane asked Amber. "You're going to risk a trip to the pet shop with this human?"

"Yes," Amber said.

"Can you really trust him?" Vervane asked in a low, secretive voice. "I mean, he *is* a human. What do we know about them?"

"Not much," Amber admitted.

"He did save me," Bushmaster reminded them. "I think he's a *good* human."

"How do we know if there even *is* such a thing as a good human?" Amber objected.

"Look at him," Vervane whispered. "There's not a hint that he ever *was* human. What he once was and what he shall become are two different things. He's a handsome mouse now. Princely even, I'd say."

Amber agreed. "Wonderfully, terribly handsome."

"I wonder," Vervane asked. "Did you make him handsome, or was he already handsome as a human?"

"I don't know," Amber replied. "Humans all look ugly to me, with all of their bald skin. I didn't think much of him, especially when he kissed me."

"He kissed you?" Vervane asked.

"Yeah," Amber said. "And when he did, I looked up his nose. It was spooky up there."

Vervane chuckled, an old man kind of chuckle. Amber laughed too, more of a schoolgirl titter.

There was a scuffling sound as Ben rolled over. Amber glanced at Ben, wondering if perhaps he'd been awake, listening to them talk about him. But he breathed evenly, and he looked as if he were asleep.

"Still," Vervane grumbled, "my heart warns that you should be careful with Ben."

"Oh, I'll be careful," Amber replied. "If he tries to bite me or tries to run away, I'll just zap him!"

"Magical powers may keep him under control," Vervane said, "but they require vigilance. In time, you'll wear yourself out trying to force him. There is a greater power at your command . . ."

"What?" Amber asked.

Bushmaster had been listening quietly, but he swiftly interjected, as if the answer were obvious, "Friendship."

"Friendship," Vervane agreed, gratified that his son had reached the conclusion so swiftly. "You want to make him your slave, and I'm sure that he will march with you for as long as you force him, but a friend would walk with you eagerly, no matter how dark the path becomes."

"I don't think he likes me much. So how do I make him a friend?"

"You do not *make* friends," Vervane said. "You can't force someone into it. Instead, you must give friendship, as the singing voles do."

"The singing voles?" Amber asked.

"They live far to the north," Vervane said, "and I have never met them, though their fame has spread wide. The singing voles live in huge cities where dozens of burrows are connected by underground tunnels.

"Sometimes, when a wolf attacks, it will try to dig through the tunnels. And that's when the voles band together to protect one another."

"How?" Amber asked.

"They sing," Bushmaster said.

"Sing?"

"Yes," Vervane offered. "They sing. While the wolf digs into one burrow, a vole will go to the mouth of another and begin to sing in a warbling voice until the wolf chases after him. Thus, he risks his life for his kin. He offers everything that he is or hopes to be. And when the wolf gives chase, the singing vole dives back into his burrow, while another on the far side of the colony goes out and takes up the song. Eventually, the wolf tires and wanders away, searching for easier prey—like a moose or a bear."

Amber fell silent.

Bushmaster said, "Those who offer their lives to their friends are called The Givvin. It's a great honor to be so named."

"I'm not giving that poopy human anything," Amber said. "Not after what his kind did to my mother and friends."

* * *

From his vantage point, Nightwing considered. He could attack Amber now. She was ignorant of the ways of magic, and that gave him an advantage. But she was also very powerful. One false move, and he could end up squashed like a mosquito on the windshield of a truck.

No, he saw something more to his liking: Ben. He wanted Ben. The human boy was filled with magic power, a vast ocean of it, just waiting for Nightwing to drain it.

But in order to get that power, he would have to break the *umbilicus magicus*, the magical connection that allowed a flow of power between Amber and Ben. Normally, he'd just have killed the wizardess in order to steal her familiar.

But Nightwing saw a safer way to handle this, a way to steal Ben away without risking his own life.

Still, I'll need help, he decided. He cast a small spell that silently sent a message to a fellow wizard, one who lived far way, near Shrew Hill. "Meet me near the freeway an hour past dawn."

Distantly, the reply came, "Yea, master, I do thy bidding."

Nightwing glanced up at the moon, and it filled him with longing.

In an effort to learn the distance to the moon, he let out a shriek in such a high pitch that even dogs couldn't hear, then counted the seconds. But no echo returned. The huntress Diana remained ever mute to his call.

He saw an opossum struggle over a fence into someone's backyard and tiptoe to a bowl of dog food while its owner snored and twitched in slumber.

Darwin the tick was asleep, sucking blood like a babe with a bottle in its mouth. One of Nightwing's veins collapsed, and Darwin began making loud sucking sounds, as if he were drawing air through a straw. The noise startled the tick from his slumber. He pulled out his proboscis. "Hey," he said, "you're a pint low! Why don't you go catch a mosquito? I could suck the blood out of it before you gobble it down."

"Because, you gore-bellied bloat," Nightwing said, "the chill night air is as void of insects as your heart is of kindness or your head is of reason."

"Why do you always insult me?" Darwin asked. "Aren't we friends?"

Nightwing shot back, "In this world, there are only two types of creatures: victims and accomplices. Be grateful, Darwin, that you are my accomplice—for now."

Grudgingly, Darwin jabbed his proboscis back into the bat, his mandibles digging in almost to Nightwing's spleen. Angered at the jab, Nightwing grabbed the tick's bloated belly and gave it a squeeze. The tick's belly was like the bulb on an eyedropper. As soon as Nightwing pinched, the blood in the tick's gut squirted back into Nightwing's veins. Immediately Nightwing felt a boost of energy.

Darwin pulled out and whined, "Hey, give that back!"

"You wanted more to drink," Nightwing said, "so drink up. It's on me—or *in* me, to be more accurate." He gave a simpering laugh and wrapped his wings around himself to conserve heat.

Dawn was coming. Nightwing hoped that Amber or Ben would show themselves before sunrise. Though he wasn't a vampire, Nightwing still feared the touch of sunlight. It made him feel vulnerable, naked somehow, and he dared not challenge a strange sorcerer beneath the sun's baleful gaze.

Rufus Flycatcher just stared at them with big bullfrog eyes.

CHAPTER 7

THE RESCUERS

Sometimes it is time to leave,
even when you don't know where you must go.
—RUFUS FLYCATCHER

As BEN LAY SLEEPING in his vole hole in Oregon, back in Louisiana, Rufus Flycatcher took timid little hops as he entered a forest deep in the bayou near Black River. The moonless night gave only the thinnest starlight, and even that was swallowed in a dense fog. He summoned a will-o'-the-wisp to light his way along a trail that was curtained by thick, gray spiderwebs. The smell of mold and death was strong in this place.

Finally, Rufus reached a small hole. His heart beat wildly as he croaked, "Howdy. Anyone home?"

He almost hoped that no one would be there.

A voice so full of murderous rage that it screamed like a buzz saw chewing through a chicken coop shot out of the hole, "What do you WANT?"

In his most innocent tone, Rufus Flycatcher called sweetly. "I, uh, just realized that it has been a coon's age since I've, uh, had the pleasure of your, uh, company, uh, Lady Blackpool."

"Oh, shut yer yap," the voice screamed, and suddenly a long gray snout came out of the hole, and Rufus stared eye to eye with the speaker—a mangy ball of fur that was quivering with rage, its left eye blinking incessantly from some nervous disorder. "Don't try to sweet talk me," the creature spat. Then her voice became low and dangerous. "*No one* ever comes to visit me unless they want something . . . *desperately*."

"Uh, yes, ma'am," Rufus rumbled. "See, the thing is, I got a whale of a problem. There's this wizardess that just bloomed into power—right in the enemy's backyard. Now, I ain't got all the details yet, but I kind of need me someone to go out and eyeball the situation fer me. You know, the usual. Save her if you can, kill her if you have to, and maybe take on an army of enemy sorcerers to boot."

"And you want me to do it *because* . . . ?" Lady Blackpool demanded.

Rufus knew what she wanted him to say, but he hesitated. He needed her precisely because she *was* a shrew. It was early spring, still, and he'd have to send someone over the Rockies. That meant that he'd need someone who was warm-blooded. He couldn't send one of the fabulous lizard wizards that roamed the swamp or an insect. He needed a bird or a mammal. None of the birds that he knew were tough enough for this job. No, it was down to the shrew or a weasel, and Rufus suspected that a mouse would be terrified of a weasel. So it was the shrew.

"You need me because?" she demanded.

Rufus gave in. "Because you're the shrewdest shrew I ever knew," he said with a groan.

"Ah, hah, hah, hah," Lady Blackpool gleefully cackled like an old witch. "That's right! That's oh so right! And what else?"

"And because you're a Ferocious Furball of Felonious Intent, and the Scariest Sorceress of the Seven Swamps."

Lady Blackpool leaped clear from her moldy hole and danced around Rufus. "Oh, Rufus, you do know the way to a lady's heart! Did you bring me a little present, my pet? Maybe something from Pappa Gumbo?"

Pappa Gumbo was the chef at SWARM, the Small Wizard's Academy of Restorative Magic, where Rufus Flycatcher served as the Headmaster. Pappa Gumbo, an enormous cockroach, was the greasiest critter in the swamps, and just maybe the finest cook in the world. As if just remembering, Rufus pulled out some treats that he'd been carrying laboriously in his little paw. "Why, I do believe . . ."

"Candied crawdads!" Lady Blackpool cried. "With slug sauce! How did he know that I had a hankerin'?"

"Pappa Gumbo always knows," Rufus said, and it was true. Papa Gumbo had a strange way of discerning what things you liked most. And if he approved of you, he would reward you accordingly. Then again, if he didn't like you much, you'd quickly find out when one of his meals took a wrong turn somewhere down in your stomach.

Lady Blackpool leaped on the candied crawdads and began chewing and salivating and making appreciative noises. Between mouthfuls, she talked as best she could. "So, do you just want me to eyeball things?"

"We don't know squat about the little lady yet," Rufus said. "Word is that she's a mouse of the snake-bait variety—straight out of a pet shop."

Lady Blackpool seemed to consider that bit of news. She stopped and gulped loudly. She fell silent, and it seemed that the night closed in, and even the curtains of cobwebs went still, as if listening. "So, she was born to be snake bait, eh? They're a barbaric lot. Uncouth, ill-mannered, ignorant of even the most basic lore of mousedom . . . Why should I save her—"

The shrew fell silent and stopped twitching for a second. That alone seemed miraculous. But then her eyes began to glow a bright magenta, and she looked to the west and focused on something miles and miles away. Rufus knew that the witch was having a vision, and she'd want to use all of her concentration to see and hear.

"I see her there," Lady Blackpool cried. "I see Amber, the Thirteenth Mouse—and the forces of darkness are gathering against her!"

The Thirteenth Mouse? Rufus wondered. That was more news than his spies had been able to obtain. Did the enemy know who she was yet?

Distantly, Rufus could hear something—the growl of thunder—and he could see lightning flashing in Lady Blackpool's eyes, as if reflected in them, and he could hear the screams of death and war, and he saw strange shadows—mice in a pitched battle, carrying weapons. "A storm is coming. A storm that will sweep the world," Lady Blackpool said.

Suddenly, the vision ended, and her glowing eyes faded to a dull purple with only the slightest hint of light. Lady Blackpool whispered desperately, "I've seen the future. I must go to her. Now."

The shrew raced past Rufus, down the trail, while curtains of cobwebs stirred in her wake. She was in such a hurry that she left her candied craw-dads.

She ran to the edge of the swamp, and Rufus followed in big hops, trying to keep up. Just where the ground surrendered to water, Lady Blackpool shouted, "Sea Foam, Lord of the Deep, I summon you!"

The water, dyed black by the tannins of cypress bark, began to swirl in a wide vortex, and waves lapped against the shore. An alligator made a burping noise and dove for cover. The water whirled faster and faster, like a whirlpool, only in reverse, for instead of sinking down, the water began to bubble above the surface, rising in a column.

Suddenly from out of the black water, an enormous sea turtle sprang up, flopping into the air.

He arced up into the trees, then dropped to the ground on his back, and lay there flapping his flippers in shock, trying to turn over.

He began to sputter, "What's . . . what's going on?"

"No time for chitchat," Lady Blackpool said. "I need help, and you owe me."

Sea Foam gulped and looked around with wide eyes.

"He owes you?" Rufus asked.

Lady Blackpool ignored the question, and Rufus suspected that he knew why. Though Lady Blackpool screamed and ranted and did much to nurture the impression that she was the wickedest witch in the swamps, she had a good heart and had probably done something to help the sea turtle at one time or another. She would just never confess to it, of course.

So instead she said in a venomous tone, "I need a ride, Sea Foam, in an armored vehicle. And you're it."

The turtle gulped and flapped his flippers helplessly. "I'll give you a swim wherever you want to go—if you'll just help flip me over."

Lady Blackpool went to the huge sea turtle, who had to weigh three hundred pounds, and flicked him with a finger of her left paw. The turtle whirled in the air and fell—splat!—on the ground. He looked about, panting, with a dazed expression.

Lady Blackpool hopped into his shell, just in the crook of his neck, and stood there muttering an incantation.

"Where to?" the poor turtle begged.

"That way!" Lady Blackpool said in a determined voice. "We're going out west. Where, I don't know, but I'll steer you true when we near the spot. Now fly!"

"Fly?" Sir Sea Foam said. "But I can't—"

"We've got a couple of thousand miles to go, with lots of crotchety weather in between and no time to get there," Lady Blackpool shouted.

"But—" Sea Foam began to say. Before he could muster another word, fire and hot gases came whooshing out of his tail hole, nearly cooking poor Rufus.

The bullfrog watched the turtle shoot into the air like a rocket and immediately begin to spin out of control. Sea Foam rose like a cannonball, screaming in fear as he spiraled toward oblivion.

In the distance, Rufus could hear Lady Blackpool shouting, "Steer, dang it! Wave those flippers!"

Sea Foam held his flippers out experimentally, and the turtle seemed to stop his wild spin.

In seconds, they were gone from sight, far out over the swamp.

Rufus Flycatcher just stared at them with big bullfrog eyes, his mouth having fallen wide open. Smoke and steam curled up from the ground beside him.

"Good-bye, Lady Blackpool," he croaked, "and vaya con Dios. You're a good-hearted woman." That last bit he said softly, not wanting her to hear. But it was true. She was the only shrew that he knew who would gleefully ride a flaming turtle through a lightning storm toward an evil army—all for a couple of Pappa Gumbo's candied crawdads. *What a woman*, he mused. *What a woman!*

The spider leaped down from its web, came close, and stared at Ben with all eight eyes.

CHAPTER 8

A GATHERING OF WEAPONS

Few critters seem to be born to be of great stature.
Instead, they become great as they rise to meet
the challenges of a dark season.
—RUFUS FLYCATCHER

BEN DREAMED THAT he was a mouse running through the morning dew, laughing at the sun, the grass-tops scrubbing his belly clean, when suddenly he realized that some terrible flying monkeys filled the sky overhead while the Wicked Witch of the West—who looked suspiciously like his mother—cackled and shouted, "Bring me Amber, and her little mouse too!"

Ben startled awake in a sweat. The voles and Amber all lay about the burrow, dead asleep. They'd worn themselves out with their singing and acrobatics.

Ben felt ravenous. He looked down at his tiny mouse's tummy. He couldn't quite figure out how so much hunger could squeeze into such a small space.

There was still food left from the night before, so Ben scrunched and nibbled a dried blueberry.

He felt utterly forlorn and wondered why. Then he remembered. He felt bad because Amber didn't trust him. She'd called him a "poopy human." He didn't deserve that. Ben fully intended to keep his part of the bargain and help her free the pet shop mice.

More than anything in the world, he *wanted* to help her, if only to win back his humanity.

He wondered how Amber would react if he shook her awake and urged her to follow him right now. Better yet, he imagined how surprised she'd be if she woke to discover that he'd already rescued the pet shop mice by himself.

But that sounded too dangerous, so he thought of another plan. He'd go and get his weapons and be all ready by the time that Amber woke.

Without another thought, Ben hopped to the magic rock, which still glowed brightly, picked it up, and tiptoed to the mouth of the burrow.

He peered out from beneath the pine needles, sniffing. The air smelled heavy with water, as if it would leave morning dew. Ben smelled pine, mold, grass, and not much more. The sun wouldn't rise for an hour.

Everything was dead quiet. No wind whispered in the morning leaves. No cars could be heard rumbling on the road.

Domino was nowhere in sight, so he scampered from the burrow toward his house. As he ran, he realized that the light that he held would show him up to any cat within a hundred yards. But he wouldn't be able to find a weapon in the dark, so he just had to tough it out.

Ben reached his property, climbed under the fence, stopped at the tree line, and checked the sky for owls. His house was on the far side of the yard. The grass hadn't been mowed all winter, and he thought about creeping through it with the light but realized it would be faster to run for it.

"Better yet, just leap *over* it, silly," Ben told himself. "You're a jumping mouse. Jump with your back feet and land on your front, like Amber does."

Ben held the rock in his mouth, gave a hard kick with his rear legs and hurtled what felt like a hundred feet in the air and four hundred feet into the distance. It was like jumping over a football field in a single bound!

As soon as he hit the grass, which bent beneath his weight like a trampoline, he bounded in the air again, kicking harder. This time he leaped what felt like two football fields.

Wow! he thought. *I really am a jumping mouse!*

Ben vaulted into the air again. *Look at me!* he thought, stretching his paws out before him. *I'm Super-vermin!*

It was the most glorious feeling that he'd ever had. It was like flying without the hassle of flapping your arms. He leaped again, doing a forward flip, and managed to get whacked in the face with the head of a wheat stalk.

He leaped again, this time doing a triple spin in the air. Thus he bounced through the yard, dodging dried weed stalks. The light showed the way. Even in the shadows, he could see the sprinkler lying in the grass and the hose coiled like a green snake. He spotted an old boot far below. As he neared the porch, he startled a sparrow hiding in the laurel bush.

He scampered to the back garage door. It was an old, weathered, wooden thing and looked as if someone had bumped it with the car. The bottom panel bent up just a bit. Ben squeezed into the garage.

It was a typical garage, big enough for two cars and with a pair of windows to let in the light. His dad's workbench filled the right wall, with lots of heavy power tools and hammers and wrenches resting on pegs above it. Shelves full of camping gear and brown boxes filled the left wall.

Next to the tent were lots of things that he couldn't use—lanterns, flashlights, a big cooler, camping stove, fishing gear, binoculars. All useless to a mouse.

A gray pill bug was crawling on the floor in front of him, tramping about on fourteen pale feet. Compared to Ben's small size, the bug looked as big as a poodle. It was giggling to itself, walking in zigzag, and muttering, "Poo-poo. Te he he. Poo-poo."

"Hello," Ben said.

"Poo-poo," it screamed and rolled itself into a ball like an armadillo, so that nothing showed but its gray armor. It looked just about the size of a soccer ball.

Ben imagined a net in the corner and kicked the bug.

"And Benjamin Ravenspell wins the World Soccer Cup again," he shouted, imagining the cheering of a billion fans around the world.

The pill bug rose high into the air, dropped toward a corner, and just stopped—in midair.

"Hey, thanks!" a deep voice called.

Ben peered into the shadows and saw a dismal web spanning from corner to corner. A dry bug, maybe a cricket, hung like a bizarre piñata at the lower end. The pill bug had hit the web. A spider was running along the strings toward the pill bug. It quickly began wrapping it into a ball.

"Hello, spider," Ben said.

"Cob. Call me Cob," the spider said.

"Are you going to eat that bug?" Ben felt guilty. He hadn't meant to kill the thing. It felt like he'd fed Amber to the lizard all over again.

"Yep," Cob said, still wrapping it tighter and tighter. "First good meal I've had all winter."

"I didn't want to hurt it," Ben said. "I wasn't trying to feed it to you."

The spider leaped down from its web, came close, and stared at Ben with all eight eyes. It was a small spider, so tiny that Ben could almost see through its carapace.

Cob said, "It's just a bug. There's not many bugs smart enough to count their own feet. That one was an intellectual giant. He could appreciate potty jokes. Yes, quite the scholar—for a pill bug."

Ben objected, "Just because it's a stupid bug doesn't mean it should be put to death."

"Too late now," the spider said, "I done injected him with my venom. He's already walked through the tunnel of light. Probably whooping it up with his pill bug ancestors. He didn't suffer none."

"Oh," Ben said. He still felt terrible. But there was nothing he could do for the bug now.

Ben held up his light and began looking for a weapon. There wasn't much here. He jumped up on the tool bench and found his dad's container of nails. The spider kept talking while Ben searched for a weapon.

"Besides," Cob hollered. "A fellow has got to eat. Been a tough winter. I sat out under the lilac bush for months. Didn't catch a danged thing in my web but a couple of snowflakes. Had some big hail last winter too—slashed my nets to shreds."

Most of the nails felt too big and heavy for Ben to carry, and the nails were really too dull to use as weapons. Ben began digging through the tin.

The spider kept talking, ignoring the fact that Ben felt uncomfortable talking to him. "Most cobs would've starved. But not me. I went on a safari. Last week, I bagged me an assassin bug. He put up quite a battle."

Ben glanced over. Cob stood a little taller. He was proud of catching that bug. Ben wasn't sure what an assassin bug was, but it sounded dangerous.

"You caught one all by yourself?" Ben asked. "Where is it?"

Cob squatted a little, deflating. "Well, uh, I tried dragging him home, but some ants caught the scent. Big old Mako fire ants, following the smell of fresh meat up from the hayfields. They kept coming at me, and I fought them off. And while I was fighting some of them off, others snuck in and grabbed pieces of my assassin bug.

"By the time I got home, all I had left was pretty much an empty shell . . ." He nodded to the piñata hanging in his web. "Yep, he was a biggun."

"I'm sorry you lost your dinner," Ben said. He glanced down. Bingo! He found a large needle, the one that his dad had bought to mend their canvas tent. "Don't be sorry for me," Cob said. "I got a little something to eat, and I had a grand adventure! You want to be sorry for someone, be sorry for the starving spiders that don't eat. I hear there's like a hundred quadrillion of 'em over in China. Hardly a fly over there to eat. Them human kung fu masters just sit around all day catching flies with their chopsticks. Don't give no never mind to other folks' needs."

Ben stood on the counter for a moment, studying his needle. A round brass doorknob nearby formed an almost perfect mirror.

Ben held the needle like a spear, as if he would jab it, and peered at his reflection. "You looking at me, cat? You looking at me? Smile when you say that!"

The spider studied Ben, then hopped a little closer. "Hey," he said, "You must be that boy who got hisself turned into a mouse."

"Y—yeah," Ben stammered. "How did you know?"

"Heard about it on the web," the spider said, as he reached out with one languid leg and plucked a silk line running across the ground. "You see, my trunk line here goes outside and connects with the widow's web under the mulberry bush. Whenever she wants to talk, she speaks into her web, and it causes the line to vibrate. Then I hear her on my side of the web. Her web connects to a burrow spider's line out back, and on and on. I can keep in touch with spiders all over town, all over the country."

"Wow," Ben said. "Us people do the same thing with computers. It's called the World Wide Web."

"Humph," the spider scoffed. "Us spiders were big on webs long before you humans figured out how to wipe your own noses."

Ben practiced a couple of thrusts with the needle. Cob moved closer to take a better look.

"So, you gonna find out what happened to all the other mice around here?" Cob asked.

"What do you mean?" Ben asked, giving the spider a sharp look.

"'Bout six months ago, they all started to disappear . . ."

Ben wondered at that. "Some voles warned me about lots of predators in the neighborhood. Maybe the cats ate them."

"That's not what I hear," Cob said. "I hear they just got up and went east, in ones or twos, wandering into the mountains. With all of the snow up there, the web was down all winter, but there's many an eye that seen 'em go."

Ben grunted. "I'll ask around."

"I like your spunk, kid," the spider said. "Word on the web is that you're out to free some mice. We spiders are taking bets. Odds are a million to one against you making it out of the pet shop alive."

"Never tell me the odds," Ben said, angrily. But he was curious. "Why so low?"

"You got enemies, kid," Cob said. "But I tell you what, I'll bet a greenbottle fly on you."

Ben took his needle in hand and hopped down from the workbench. There was a bag of walnuts in a corner, so he went to it, dug through the shells, and found one to use as a helmet. He put it on, but it kept popping off. He finally got it to stick in place, sort of, by scrunching his ears just right, then went to his dad's fishing pole, lying on the floor. It had a size 14 egg hook on it—three little golden hooks really, welded together into a triangle. It kind of looked like a grappling hook. Ben bit off six feet of leader, coiled it like a rope, and clutched it in one paw.

"Now any cat that tries to eat me will get a hook caught in its mouth," Ben said. It was hard to carry everything—the light, the grappling hook, the spear.

"Hey, looks like you could use a couple of extra legs," Cob said. "I'd gladly give you a pair of mine. Never could figure out what to do with all of 'em."

"Thanks for the offer," Ben said. "Good-bye, Cob."

"Bye," Cob said.

Ben dove through the hole under the door, and as he did, he became aware of a huge fuzzy shadow overhead. Something pounced, then grasped him cruelly, knocking the spear from his hand, along with his grappling hook and light.

There, in the garish green glow thrown by the magic stone, Ben saw an enormous raccoon, its evil eyes glinting behind its black mask, its gray grizzled fur sticking out everywhere. It hunched over him, larger than the Sphinx. Its claws were longer than the blade of a scythe, and its cruel teeth were each sharper than spears.

"Gotcha!" the raccoon said.

Ben's heart pounded a thousand times a minute, and he felt sick all over. A moment ago, he'd felt so safe, and now all of his weapons were gone, useless. His mind went blank as he tried to consider what to do.

Buy time, he thought. The raccoon pulled Ben up toward its mouth, using a finger to flick Ben's walnut shell helmet from his head. The helmet went plunking to the ground.

"Aren't you going to wash before you eat me?" Ben asked. "I thought raccoons always washed first."

"Not if we're hungry enough," the coon said, shoving Ben eagerly toward his mouth.

"Oh," Ben said. "Then I'm *dreadfully* sorry."

The raccoon stopped, eyeing him curiously. "Sorry for what?"

"I think . . . I think . . . I think I just pooped in your paw."

The raccoon screamed, hurling Ben to the ground. The beast held up its paws as if they had been burned.

Ben hit the pavement rolling. He grabbed his needle, somersaulted, and came up with it at the ready. With one free paw, he grabbed up his helmet and jammed it onto his head, then held it in place.

The raccoon was staring at its paws in horror. "Hey," it said, "you didn't poop!"

Ben menaced the giant with his spear. "You want a piece of me? Go ahead, make my day!"

The raccoon backed up an inch, then seemed to find his courage. "Hey, I ain't afraid of no mouse!"

"Hay is for horses," Ben shouted, leaping three feet into the air. "Hyaaah!" He plunged his spear deep into the raccoon's snout,

The raccoon let out a startled cry, blinked, and stepped back a pace.

Ben suddenly remembered something his neighbor, Mrs. Pumpernickle, had said last winter. She'd said that she'd gone out on the porch one night, and a big raccoon had been in the garbage. She tried to drive it away, but it had merely growled and snapped at her.

As the raccoon squared off, Ben realized that this was probably the same monster.

The raccoon laughed. "A spunky one, eh? You don't scare me. I eat *live* scorpions as treats and wash 'em down with glue!"

He was stalking toward Ben when a dark shadow dropped from the top of the pine tree.

"Owl," Ben shouted, imagining that he'd have to fight two predators at once. Things couldn't get worse.

But what twisted through the air was no owl. Ben could sense something powerful and malevolent rushing toward him. It came with the force of a bullet, but wriggled like a bat.

Time seemed to stop, and Ben watched it draw near in slow motion. Its thick orange fur glowed sullenly by Ben's magic light, as if revealing some inner fire. Its enormous ears, so translucent that one could see the veins, were each fully six times as long as its pug-nosed head. Its yellow teeth were as sharp as nails. The ear studs and magical symbols tattooed onto its ears lent the creature a terrifying sense of power. It was, by far, the most hideous creature that Ben had ever seen.

He couldn't have been more frightened if he saw the devil himself winging his way out of the underworld.

The bat landed next to Ben and stood with the tiny claws of its wings hooked to the ground, then twisted its head around to look at the raccoon. It bared its teeth and hissed.

"Your *Mage*-esty," the raccoon cried. It dropped its head low, bowing and backing off a step. "I didn't mean to—is he a friend of yours?—I mean forgive me, I, uh—"

"Get out of here," the bat said, "before I make you beg me to chew your own tail off."

The raccoon shouted and bolted around the side of the house so fast that the only thing left of him was his stink and a couple of hairs that floated in the wind.

The bat chuckled, low and dangerously.

Ben was horrified. His hands felt weak. It took all of his effort to grip his spear. He suspected that normal weapons were worthless against this monster.

"Well done," the creature hissed. "You showed courage and initiative."

Ben's eyes grew wide. "What are you? Some kind of weird bat?"

"Some might call me a bat, but I prefer to think of myself as a Dusky Seraph," the bat said.

"Oh," Ben said. "Do you have a name?"

"My friends call me Nightwing."

Ben heard a sucking sound and noticed a horrible fat tick with its head buried in the bat's armpit. The tick pulled its head out. "I didn't know you had friends. I thought you said that the world was divided into *accomplices* and *victims*."

"Quiet," Nightwing said, and the tick's proboscis suddenly cinched tight, as if an invisible string were wrapped around it. Muffled screams came from the now-closed proboscis.

The bat hobbled around Ben, stalking on tiny paws, using his wings to balance. "Impressive," Nightwing said. "Very impressive. A jumping mouse, but strangely dressed. Or are you more than you seem?"

"I'm a human," Ben said proudly. "Or I was. Until I got turned into a mouse."

Quick as thought, Nightwing reached out and put a claw around Ben's shoulder. "Well, then, you and I have something in common!"

Ben eyed the bat distrustfully.

The bat peered hard at Ben, and then squinted skyward as if he longed to seek the shelter of the shadowed pines. The rising sun seemed a threat. The bat smiled and drooped his ears. Suddenly he seemed smaller and not so menacing as he squinted at Ben like a kindly, half-blind old man. "For you see, I too was once a human. A man of some importance. A celebrity. I was, how do you young ones say it, 'the cat's slumber-wear.'"

"Really?" Ben said. "Who?"

The bat looked away sadly. "It's not important. It was so long ago. I remember so little now. I . . . I was a man of great intellect, a lighthouse at the end of the world. Crowds came out of the shadows to peer at me and wonder at my brilliance. I would speak syllables into the air, filling auditoriums with the music of my voice. I was the man who put the Poe in poetry. Ah, how women would look upon me in ardor and swoon!" Nightwing paused and let out a sigh. "But I remember so little. That's how it is when you have been transmogrified. The longer you stay in your new form, the harder it becomes to remember what it was to be human . . ."

"Oh," Ben said, wondering. Would he be like this bat someday, incapable of remembering his own name? Already he felt something of what it was like to be a mouse—to have a mouse's hunger, a mouse's fears.

"I know a wizardess," Ben offered. "Maybe she could turn you back into a human."

Tears suddenly brimmed from the bat's eyes. He seemed as if he did not know how to respond, as if such a boon were beyond his wildest dreams, or as if it had been countless ages since anyone had shown him a kindness. "Really? She could do that?"

"She's the one who turned me into a mouse."

"Tell me about it," Nightwing begged, and Ben found the story tumbling out of him like clothes from an open dryer. Though he wanted to hold a few things back, he felt compelled, as if some spell forced him to speak. So he told Nightwing how Amber had turned him into a mouse and how she had promised to restore him to his human form if he would only help free the pet shop mice.

When he finished, he was breathing hard. Nightwing reached up and put a pitying claw on Ben's shoulder. "I can tell that you and I are going to be good friends. Perhaps we can be of help to one another."

"How?" Ben asked.

"I must confess," Nightwing said. "I know a bit about sorcery, too. And I have some suspicions. I believe, dear boy, that you yourself may hold the key to Amber's magical power."

"What do you mean?"

"Well," Nightwing drew nearer. "This mouse of yours, Amber, has never done any magic before, you said?"

"No," Ben replied. "I guess not."

"Until she met *you.* And now she's casting powerful spells indeed. Doesn't that strike you as odd?"

"I hadn't thought about it," Ben admitted.

"Well, I find that very odd. For you see, in order to cast a spell, one needs power, and the source of that power is an invisible element. Let's call it *mage dust.* It's the source of magic, and it is all around us—in the air, on the ground, on you. You can't see it. Can't smell it. But some folks attract it the way that magnets attract iron filings. When they walk about, the mage dust sticks to them the way that burrs or dirt stick to your fur. Such folks may not be magicians themselves, but they're still immensely powerful. They provide the fuel for the magician's fires. They're called *familiars.*"

"Oh," Ben said. He suddenly understood what the bat was getting at. Ben felt so shocked, he fell backward, tripping over his tail. He climbed to his knees, "You think *I'm* a familiar? I . . . I store magic power?"

"It makes sense," the bat said. "Amber, you see, was born in a cage and never got out. So she couldn't gather any power, any mage dust. And when she went to your house, she suddenly cast powerful spells indeed. Where did she get that power? It's not likely that she got it just by taking a short drive. No, you must have been storing mage dust your whole life in order for her to cast such a spell."

Ben shivered at the thought. "So, I'm like a battery?"

"Yes," Nightwing said slyly. "And therein lies the danger. Every time she casts a spell, she drains you a little. And performing a spell like a transmogrification requires enormous amounts of power."

"Uh-huh," Ben said.

"Which means," Nightwing said pointedly, "that if she's ever going to turn us back into people, she has to stop using magic immediately."

"Oh no," Ben cried. "I'd better tell her!"

"Do you trust her that much?" Nightwing asked slyly with a sour expression that suggested that he shouldn't trust her at all.

"She seems nice enough."

"Yes," Nightwing said. "But what will happen when she learns that you are the source of her power? Do you really think she'll turn you back into a human? Would she let you go, leaving herself a weak little mouse, just another snack for the cats?"

Ben suddenly felt very worried indeed. No, of course she wouldn't free him. Not if she knew the truth.

"What can I do?" Ben asked.

Nightwing seemed to think for a moment. "Don't tell her anything. Don't let her know that you are the source of her power. Let her turn you back into a human. And if she doesn't keep her word, look for a chance to escape and then just run away. There is a place you can go, a school for wizards, called the Small Animal's Darling Institute of Sorcerous Technology, or SADIST, for short. The legendary Wizards of the Coast study there. All you have to do is head due west from here, only a few dozen miles. Perhaps they will turn you back into a human . . ."

Ben made a mental note: SADIST, to the west. Then the bat looked up at the fading darkness and leaped into the air, his wings creaking like rusty hinges as he flew toward the shadowed fir trees. He dipped among their limbs and was lost to Ben's view.

Hop, stop, and look, six eyes peering warily.

CHAPTER 9

DREAMS OF MICE AND MEADOWS

If we shadows have offended,
Think but this, and all is mended:
That you have but slumbered here,
While these visions did appear.
—WILLIAM SHAKESPEARE

IN THE SHADOWS of the lonesome trees, Nightwing had a moment to reflect. He hid in the tallest Douglas fir and enjoyed the feel of the tree swaying, its sweet scent filling his nostrils.

He felt comfortable in the shadows.

Let's see, he thought. *I've planted seeds of discord with Ben. Now all that I need to do is trick Amber, and Ben will be mine.*

I know, a dream! A dream just might do the trick . . .

* * *

Amber lay in a deep slumber in the voles' burrow, and suddenly her body jerked. Her eyes came half open, but her eyelids were too heavy, and soon they dropped.

In the warm darkness, filled with the sweet scent of the friendly voles, Amber dreamed.

She dreamed that she heard Ben calling her name from a distance, as if he needed her, and in her dream, she climbed to her feet and sniffed through the burrow.

Suddenly, there was a light in a tunnel, and Ben entered—wearing a walnut shell upon his head and carrying a sharp piece of metal in one paw and the glow-stone in the other. A silver thread with a golden hook tied to it was slung over one shoulder.

"Amber," he called desperately, "there you are!"

She gazed upon him, and no mouse of the field had ever looked so handsome. His glossy fur had been preened and stroked to a soft gleam. His eyes were as bright as stars in the darkness. Amber's stomach felt all gooey.

Ben rushed forward. For a moment he stared at her lovingly. "What have I been thinking?" he whispered, inching forward to nuzzle her ear. "I don't want to leave. I want to be with you. Forever. I want to be yours."

Amber's heart thrilled. She quivered with excitement. "Really?"

"Amber, without you," Ben said, "there could be no magic in my life. There could be no magic in your life. Think about it—you never could cast a spell until you met me. We're like two halves of a peanut. Together we are magic. Alone, we're just . . . nuts."

Amber stood quivering, not knowing what to say. Ben leaned forward, his whiskers trembling. He sniffed her ear. It tickled. She giggled, wondering if he really loved her.

He did kiss me, she told herself. *Even when he was a human, he kissed me. He must love me a little.*

She wanted him to love her so badly that it hurt.

* * *

After a long, deep sleep, Amber woke in pain. Not pain in her muscles, but pain in her heart, aching for Ben.

Vervane scurried about the burrow shouting, "Rise my friends. Rise. The night is old; the stars are dim. The owls have gone to roost, and the hawks have not yet awakened. Hurry. Now is the time to travel!"

Amber blinked in surprise. She'd expected to find Ben nuzzling her. But she felt cold, alone.

The scents of fungi, leaves, and voles were strong. Amber rubbed her eyes. Her magical light was gone. She heard young voles rustling about the burrow.

The burrow! For the first time in her life, she had wakened to life outside a cage. She really was free!

I'll never go back to a cage, she vowed.

Amber needed light, so she wished that she had another glowing rock. A nearby pebble flickered like an ember, then went out.

Amber suddenly felt weak. She fell to her belly and lay as slack as a slug. Something was wrong.

She lay, head spinning, listening to the voices in the burrow. Suddenly, she realized that she hadn't heard Ben.

"Ben?" she called weakly. "Ben?" Now she saw the truth. Ben had run away with her glow-stone.

She felt betrayed. In her dream, he had been so loving, so tender. Now, fear wormed through her belly. She didn't know how to find the pet shop without Ben. And there would be monsters all along the way.

I was such a fool to trust him, Amber thought.

Just as she began to cry, a light shone at one end of the burrow, and Ben crawled into view. He was wearing the walnut shell on his head and carrying a long piece of metal in one hand and the glow-stone in the other—just as he had in her dream!

In the dark, his eyes sparkled like droplets of water.

And as he neared, something strange happened. The stone that Amber had tried to make glow suddenly turned as clear as glass and flared like a star.

Amber gasped as she realized that her dream had held some truth—she couldn't do magic without Ben. They *were* two halves of the same peanut. They were magic only when they were together.

And what of the rest of the dream? Amber wondered. *Was there truth in it, too? Is it possible that he really does love me, that he wants to be a mouse?*

Old Barley Beard had once told Amber, "Sometimes we can see truths clearly in dreams that we are blind to while awake." Maybe Barley Beard had been right.

Ben's very presence seemed to revitalize Amber, to send strength pulsing through her limbs. She climbed to her feet. Trying to keep the sound of her fear and hurt from her voice, she asked Ben, "Where did you go?"

"Uh," Ben said. "I wanted to get an early start on our trip, so I went back to get some weapons."

"What's a weapon?" Bushmaster asked. The vole drew near, sniffed at the spike that Ben held. "Is that it?"

"It's something we humans use to fight with," Ben said. He picked it up and showed the vole how to thrust and jab with it. "With one of these, you can beat up cats and stuff."

Amber didn't believe such wild tales, but Bushmaster drew close. "There's blood on it. And I smell raccoon!"

"Yeah," Ben said. "I almost got eaten by one. But I stabbed him in the nose, and he ran away."

The voles stared at Ben in awe, mouths falling open.

Vervane came and sniffed at Ben's spear. With a sound approaching worshipfulness, he asked, "You fought a raccoon?"

"Yeah," Ben said. "I got this needle out of the garage to use as a spear. But you could use a nail or a toothpick—anything that's sharp. In fact, if you get into someone's house, there's always a good chance of finding a needle somewhere."

Ben tried to hand the spear to Vervane, but the old vole backed away. "No, no, thank you," he shuddered. "I could never *kill* anything."

But Bushmaster hopped forward, picked up the spear, and tried a couple of jabs. He began laughing at his newfound sense of power. "I want one!" he said. "We don't really have to *kill* things. We could just use them to scare monsters off."

"I never thought of that," Vervane admitted. "Maybe I *could* use one."

"Me, too!" the younger voles all cried.

In seconds, the voles were crowding around Ben, talking excitedly, making plans to search every home in the neighborhood for weapons.

They gaped at the walnut shell on Ben's head. "What's that for?" one asked.

"It's a helmet," Ben said. "It protects your head. A cat would have a hard time biting through it."

One vole touched it, and the walnut shell popped off of Ben's head.

Ben looked down at it sadly. "It keeps coming off. If I had a knife, I'd whittle on it until it fit. I'd make it look cool, like a scary skull with teeth and stuff!"

Amber went to Ben and picked up the walnut shell. She imagined the scariest thing she could—the walnut shell carved to look like bone, with holes for Ben's eyes and ears and teeth wrapping down over his jaws to hold the helmet on.

Immediately, the walnut shell took the new form. The voles all squeaked in fear and backed away.

"A princely helm for a princely mouse," Amber said.

"Cool," Ben said, slapping it on.

With a wave of her paw, Amber gathered all of the needles from Ben's house and let them form in the air. They dropped at the feet of the voles. "A present," she said. "Here are weapons for all of you, so that Domino the cat will learn to fear the small creatures of the world!"

"Yay!" the voles all cried as they selected their weapons. "Hooray for Amber! Hooray for Ben!"

"So how far is the pet shop?" Amber asked Ben as the voles continued to cheer. "And which way do we go?"

"The sun rises in the east," Ben said. "All we have to do is follow it."

"Great!" Amber said. "What's the sun?"

"You know," Ben said in exasperation, "they really should have let you out of your cage more often."

Bushmaster hopped close to Ben. "Between your weapons and her spells, nothing can stop us. All we have to do is get both of you to the pet shop, and you'll be human in no time."

"Wait a minute," Ben suddenly asked Bushmaster, "are *you* coming too?"

"It's the least I can do," Bushmaster said. "You saved my life. Besides, six eyes watching for monsters are better than four. And now I have a spear!"

Old Vervane laughed. "Bushmaster always was the adventurous one. He knows every backyard from here to the end of the block."

Somehow, the news that Bushmaster would come made Amber feel better. Bushmaster was only a vole, but he was a wild vole, and he knew how to travel through dangerous country filled with monsters that she'd never dreamed of.

The voles began shouting farewells, and with that, Bushmaster picked up his spear and led the way from the burrow.

"Travel safely," the young girl Meadowsweet called. "Come back soon."

"Thank you," Amber told her. "I'd love to."

Ben dropped the magic light-stone, muttering, "We'll have to leave this. It would only attract attention."

Amber threaded her way out of the burrow, just behind Bushmaster, and glanced back longingly at her magic lights. They dimmed as she left.

At their backs, the youngest voles teased, "Good-bye, mice! Good-bye, stinky mice!" They giggled and rolled on the floor while their older kin gathered up the spears.

* * *

At the top of the burrow, Ben took the lead. It was still dark, with just a hint of light. The scents of trees and bushes and moist earth clung to the ground. Ben climbed from the hole and shoved aside a young fern that spiraled up out of the humus. He trudged forward blindly into the pre-dawn gloom with spear in hand.

"What are you doing?" Bushmaster cried in horror.

"Heading to the pet shop," Ben said as he stomped over the pine needles, climbing toward a large yellow oyster mushroom that glowed in the shadows ahead.

"You can't just march around like that," Bushmaster argued. "You have to be careful. Hop, stop, and look. Hop, stop, and look."

"At that rate, it will take all day," Ben argued.

"Perhaps," Bushmaster said, "but remember, the shortest distance between two points is getting there alive."

Ben said impatiently, "My teacher says that the shortest distance between two points is a straight line."

Bushmaster grunted in disgust. "I'd like to see your teacher walk a straight line through a field of weasels."

"All right," Ben said. Ben hopped forward a few steps, hid beneath a wild daffodil, and made a big show of peering around. "Whew," he groused. "I made it two feet alive. Hope I can keep it up." He darted forward three hops—enormous bounds that only a jumping mouse could manage—and pretended to evade an owl, zigzagging until he reached a pile of pine needles. Amber's anger started to rise, but she kept her mouth shut.

East took them away from Ben's house, through a stand of fir trees, and down a rolling hill. In the predawn, it was spooky. The shriek of some hunting bird shattered the darkness, and every shadow under every crooked bush and crouching tree was filled with menace.

Vapors rose from the ground, like the ghosts of woodlands past, and broken limbs on the forest floor seemed to twist like dazed snakes. The mice climbed down into a valley where green moss grew and mushrooms sprouted from the moss, white as snow.

Amber trembled in fear as she wound her way beneath the umbrella tops of the mushrooms. She considered her plan. Old Barley Beard had told her that she was destined to free all of the mice in the world someday.

Today is the day, she thought. *I'll reach the pet shop and free my friends, fulfilling the prophecy.*

But in doing so, she'd lose Ben.

Will I never be able to use magic again after that? she wondered. It seemed unlikely.

Amber had to come to grips with the fact that once Ben was human, she'd just be a common house mouse. *Or at least one with a spear*, she mused, grinning wickedly.

As dawn filled the sky, the sense of menace faded and the world displayed its wonders. They reached the edge of a meadow—a real meadow, just like old Barley Beard had dreamed of. There, the mice climbed a small madrone tree, whose peeling red bark revealed a honey-colored layer of pith beneath, and sat under its waxy green leaves as Amber took her first good look at the world.

The meadow was filled with lush green grass, morning glories opening their white petals to the world, golden daffodils, and wild mountain blue irises springing from the ground.

In the distance, Amber could see a shining disk, rising pink above the purple mountains and the morning fog that filled the Willamette Valley.

"That's the sun," Ben said. "We just head toward it."

Oh, Amber thought. It was like a lightbulb back in the pet shop, only this one brightened the whole world.

Down in the meadow, her eyes caught the movement of animals. She saw cottontail bunnies bouncing playfully at the tree line, and by a small pool of water, a stately animal stood. It had some branches stuck on its head.

"What's that?" she asked.

"It's a deer," Bushmaster said, "with his antlers in velvet. With rabbits and deer in the meadow, that's a good sign. There shouldn't be any predators around."

"Hooray," Amber cried.

"We should have a song," Bushmaster said, "to give us peace of mind on our journey." And so he sat on the limb beneath the bush and sang in a loud, clear voice:

The trail is long and lonely,
And soon I'll reach the end,
In sunlight or in shadow,
I'll come to you, my friend.

When death is at your doorway,
And there's no one to defend
In day or utter darkness,
I'll stand with you, my friend.
In day or utter darkness,
I'll sing for you, my friend.

Amber took a long look at Bushmaster. "That's a song from the singing voles of the north, isn't it?"

"Yes," Bushmaster said. "It's what they sing when a friend is in danger."

They sat for a moment, looking out over the meadow. It was early spring, and as the morning light eased through the trees, birdsong trembled in the air. Indeed, birds were everywhere. Golden meadowlarks erupted from the fescue like hot sparks from a forge; while hidden, they whistled songs both sweet and haunting. Red-winged blackbirds clung to the tops of cattail rushes along a small stream, making ratcheting noises as they hunted for caterpillars and bees. Finches and sparrows hopped in the brush at the edge of the woods, cheeping. And suddenly, far, far up, Bushmaster spotted a red-winged hawk wheeling in lazy circles through the sky.

"Time to get under cover," he whispered, hopping to the ground.

The mice furtively crept through the grass, Ben taking the lead with his spear in hand, Amber in the middle, Bushmaster following at the end. The thick grass slowed them. Rye and fescue and wild vetch all competed for sunlight and grew in a tangled jungle. There were trails—hidden runways for small creatures—but the erratic paths often didn't head the direction that they needed to go.

"Who made these trails?" Ben asked as they nosed through some thick grass. "Mice?"

"Not likely," Bushmaster said. "The mice have all gone away. Voles are making these trails, mostly."

"So they should be safe to follow?" Ben asked.

"Others use them," Bushmaster said. "Pine snakes and garter snakes like to slither along them, and weasels. We have to be careful, even on the trails."

Amber was curious. "You said the mice went away. Where did they go?"

"East," Bushmaster said. "They went east. I asked, but they didn't know where they were heading, or why they were leaving. Sometimes they muttered, 'Into the Shadow,' but they couldn't tell me where the Shadow was or why they wanted to get there. They left in ones and twos, the mothers leading their kittens."

"Did you humans notice this?" Amber asked Ben.

Ben shook his head.

Amber crept along silently, wondering what this could mean. The only animals she saw were small creatures—wolf spiders trundling along the grass, ants hunting in huge tribes, snails as round and pale as the moon, bright red ladybugs dozing in the dawn, a young mantis praying fervently for world peace.

So they nosed through the grass, panting and grunting, until they got hungry.

For the first time in her life, Amber foraged for oats and clover. She drank morning dew from golden buttercups, dined on wild peas. It seemed to her to be the finest feast she'd ever eaten.

* * *

Dave Hugely, owner of Noah's Ark Pet Shop, always found his pulse racing just a bit when a customer walked into the store with a cardboard box. It was just like Christmas. You never knew what might be hidden in the package. Usually, it was just a dozen ugly calico kittens or a green iguana that had grown too big for its cage. But sometimes the box held real treasures—like the time a fellow brought in an albino cobra.

"Thing's eatin' three rats a week," the fellow had complained.

"Well," Dave had hemmed and hawed. "I don't know what I'd do with a big, old poison snake. Can't sell 'em, legally."

"Maybe you could find a home for it . . . sort of on the side," the fellow had suggested.

"Tell you what," Dave offered. "I could take him off of your hands for you. Maybe even give you twenty bucks."

And he bought himself a twelve-foot-long albino cobra.

Now, few people knew it, but Dave really ran *two* pet shops. There was the Noah's Ark that all of the mothers and children in the neighborhood knew and loved—home to clown fish and love-birds and sweet little puppies with their slobbery tongues.

Then there was the *secret* pet shop in the back room where Dave kept his more creepy pets—giant piranhas from Venezuela, a mating pair of Komodo dragons, Egyptian pygmy owls that were a huge hit with the Harry Potter crowd, snakehead fish out of Thailand, baby crocodiles, frilled lizards from the outback, and a Colombian anaconda large enough to swallow a child whole, just to name a few.

That's where Dave made his big money, selling the bizarre, the dangerous, the illegal. And so when he got his albino cobra, it had been a real treasure. He'd sold it to a doctor in China, where it was dried in the sun and ground up for love potions. A dandy like that one was worth $10,000 a pound.

So Dave got excited that morning when he saw a disreputable-looking fellow carrying a plain cardboard box.

The guy hung off to the back of the store, waited until some kids finished petting the spaniel puppies and then left the shop.

"What you got in the box?" Dave asked as soon as they were alone.

The guy's voice was husky. "I don't rightly know." With trembling hands, he began to open the box. Usually when a customer didn't know what he had, it meant that it was some off-breed cat or dog. Something rare. Dave would pretend it was a mutt, buy it for practically nothing, and then auction it off on eBay.

But as soon as this fellow opened the box, Dave jumped away. It wasn't a mutt. It was a monster!

"What the devil do you think it is?" the fellow asked.

Dave peered into the box, and moved to the side. The customer was shaking.

"I mean, it kind of looks like a . . . uh, like a porcupine, with an octopus stuck on its face."

"Yeah," Dave agreed. "Maybe with a little badger thrown in. Got mean teeth. But look at that tail."

Dave had never seen anything like it. The creature wasn't huge—not much bigger than a cottontail rabbit. And it didn't seem to be healthy. It just lay in the box as if it were nearly dead. In fact, Dave would have thought it was a fake—like those little jackalope heads that the local taxidermists made for tourists by mounting deer antlers onto a stuffed rabbit. But this creature was definitely breathing and peering around.

Porcupine body. Octopus with tentacles for a face. A spiked tail, kind of like an otter. Webbed feet, sharp claws, and teeth. Two small eyes on the right side of its head, one above the other. But only one big eye on the left.

And the stink! *By golly*, Dave thought, *last time I smelled anything that bad was when I accidentally left that big old can of fishing worms in the refrigerator for a month.*

"Where did you get it?" Dave asked.

"Up in the mountains on the coast," the customer said. "I've been trapping coyotes up in Hells Canyon, just below Shrew Hill. I was running my traplines this morning, and this fellow crawled up on the side of the road. He stood on his back legs and just waved them tentacles at me, almost like he was trying to flag me down."

It was odd—and creepy. Dave had heard tales of strange creatures up by Shrew Hill.

"You know," Dave surmised. "I think I know what this is. It looks to me like a star-nosed mole, kind of. You know, one of those moles with the pink fingers on its nose that eats worms and slugs?"

"Kind of," the customer admitted, dubiously.

"Yeah," Dave suggested, "that's what it is. Except that it's giant, and the tentacles are way too long. It must be some kind of . . . well, a mutant?"

At that, the animal changed colors almost instantly. The pink tentacles suddenly went dark red, then deep blue.

"Lots of weird animals up at Shrew Hill," the trapper said. "I've heard tales of Sasquatches."

"Now, that I'd like to see," Dave said. "You bring me a Sasquatch, and it might be worth something."

"I've seen things too," the trapper admitted. His voice was frightened and husky, as if he didn't really want to speak. "I saw a mountain sheep up there four days ago. Had a head on it like a little girl. Pretty girl, with blonde hair and dark brown doe's eyes. I pulled out my pistol and was gonna shoot her, but she just kept smiling at me and munching on a raspberry bush."

Dave just stared at the trapper. He sniffed the air, to see if the fellow had been drinking. "You know," Dave offered, "maybe this is more of a half-breed. Kind of like a star-nosed mole mixed with a porcupine."

"Yeah," the fellow suggested.

"There's all kinds of strange things like this in the world," Dave said. "There were some fox hunters out in Iowa last year, shot something that looked like a rabbit with long fangs. They caught it eating a sheep."

"Yeah," the customer said. "Or like that girl in Brazil a few years back, who went swimming in the pond—"

"And had that baby that was half-frog!" Dave finished. He tried to force the image from his mind. He'd seen the pictures—a pathetic boy with webbed fingers and toes and enormous milky eyes. They'd said that his tongue was as long as a belt.

"Yeah," the customer said. "Whatever happened to him, anyway?"

Dave made a tsking sound. "I heard that he croaked."

The customer laughed. "Well, with his parentage, it was bound to happen."

Dave had the customer in a good mood. Now all that he had to do was convince the trapper that the creature was worthless. The fellow was chewing tobacco and suddenly realized that he had to spit. He looked around the pet shop, as if Dave might have a spittoon. But when he didn't see one, he ducked his head and spat into the front pocket of his Levi shirt.

"You know," Dave said. "I have a friend who teaches at Oregon State University. He could probably do some DNA tests and figure out what this thing is." Dave liked that angle. It made it sound as if he was going to give the creature up for science, even though museums often paid big bucks for something like this.

The customer sort of held back. He'd been hoping for money. "I don't know . . ." the fellow said.

"What do you think it eats?" Dave asked. "I mean, it doesn't look too healthy."

The guy shrugged. Dave liked playing on the customer's fears, suggesting that the animal would die without his expertise. "Tell you what," Dave offered. "I'll give you . . . twenty bucks for it."

"I was thinking a couple hundred," the trapper suggested.

Dave smiled inwardly. Even if he paid a couple hundred, he ought to do well on the trade. "You know, this is a wild animal," he said. "Maybe it's even some rare species, one of a kind. We might get a big fine if we got caught with it. Tell you what, why don't you take it over to the Fish and Game Department first and ask them? Maybe they can tell you what it is."

The customer visibly paled, imagining huge fines and small prison cells. Those guys at the Fish and Game Department could bankrupt you just for looking wrong at a wild animal. "You'll give me twenty bucks?"

Dave thought for a long minute. "On second thought, I'd better not. You go ahead and keep it."

"Maybe," the customer suggested, now only wanting to escape, "you could take it to that professor of yours and see what he says. I mean, he's a scientist, right? He's probably got some kind of permit for critters like this."

Dave didn't want to sound too eager. He backed off. "I'll tell you what. I'll put it in the back room and give my friend a call. If he can take it off our hands, I'll let him. But if he can't, I'll give you a call, and you've gotta come pick it up right away."

"Okay," the customer said nervously. The fellow immediately changed the subject, pretending that he was interested in buying a long-horned chameleon, but Dave didn't fail to notice that he practically ran out of the store without offering his phone number.

And without it, there was no way that Dave could contact the customer to pay him for the monster, even if he wanted to.

With a wide grin, Dave took the monster into the back room, looking for a cage strong enough to hold it.

Maybe, he thought, *I'll just give that Chinese doctor a call . . .*

* * *

As the mice rested beneath some swordtail ferns to let their breakfast digest, Ben said, "You know, I've never felt so starved. Do mice always get this hungry?"

"You know what they say," Bushmaster offered, "'To keep hunger away, eat half your weight in food each day.'"

Ben laughed. "Half my weight? That would be forty pounds when I was a human. Do you mice have any other sayings?"

"Like what?" Bushmaster asked.

"I don't know . . . like 'Be as quiet as a mouse'?"

"That's silly," Amber replied. "Mice can make quite a racket. Mother always told me to 'Be as quiet as a rock.'"

"Hmmm . . ." Ben said. "What about 'The bigger they are, the harder they fall'?"

"That's backward," Bushmaster responded. "We voles say 'The bigger they are, the easier it is for 'em to squish us.' And if you don't believe me, wait until you've been trampled by a herd of rampaging chipmunks!"

Amber didn't want to say it, but human truisms didn't make much sense. Rocks were much quieter than mice. And she'd sure hate to get run over by a chipmunk. Amber had always thought that humans must be smart because of all the stuff they made. But Ben sounded incredibly naive. Maybe it was because he was only a child, she reasoned.

"Ben," Amber asked, "how old are you?"

"Ten," Ben answered.

"Really?" she said. "I'm ten weeks old too!"

"No," Ben said. "Ten *years*."

Amber's mind did a flip.

"Whoa!" Bushmaster said. "Ten whole years? That's like, forever! I'm only four *months* old."

"Wait a minute," Ben asked, "how long do mice live?"

"A year, maybe two—if you're lucky," Amber said.

"Then . . . if I'm a mouse, does that mean I'm aging as fast as a mouse?" Ben asked.

"Of course," Amber said.

"Then a mouse's week is about the same as a human's year. And a day is like . . ."

"Two months?" Bushmaster suggested.

"If you stay a mouse, you'll be fully grown in a month," Amber said. "And you'll be ready to get married. Wouldn't that be nice?"

Ben wheeled, gripping his spear tightly. "Is that what you want? You want to marry me? Is that why you want me to stay a mouse?" He trembled with rage, and his voice was thick with disgust.

"No," Amber said, hoping to calm him.

"I heard you talking to Vervane," Ben accused. "You think I'm terribly handsome."

Amber felt hurt. "I only meant it as a compliment," Amber said. "Don't you think I'm pretty?"

Ben spat an insult. "I think you look like the poster girl for D-Con rat poison!"

D-Con. That must be the poison they use to kill us mice with, Amber realized. She felt flustered and hurt. "You may be terribly handsome on the outside," Amber said. "But I think you're just *terrible* on the inside."

"Yeah?" Ben said. "Who cares what a vermin thinks?"

That was twice that Amber had heard the word *vermin*. It wasn't a word that she'd learned at the pet shop, so she wished that she knew the meaning, and suddenly she understood. It was a human word, from an ancient group of people called the Romans, and it meant a *worm*, like the worms that lived in people's guts. It was about the most disgusting thing that Ben could have called her.

"Amber's a pretty mouse," Bushmaster said. "If I were a mouse, I'd marry her in a heartbeat."

"Maybe *you* should," Ben said, "but I've got a better idea." He wheeled on Amber. "Turn me into a human, and I'll carry you to the pet shop. We can be there in no time."

He sounded desperate. Every minute that he stayed a mouse, hours of his life were slipping away.

Amber demanded, "How do I know that you'll keep your bargain once I turn you into a human?"

"If I don't," Ben said, "you can always turn me back into a mouse again."

Amber felt uneasy. Was being a mouse really so bad?

She really didn't want to lose Ben. His presence comforted her. He was ten years old, after all, and was filled with ancient wisdom. And he was strong. What other mouse knew how to use weapons?

There was a lot that she could learn from him. And though she hardly dared admit it even to herself, he *was* handsome. Dreamily handsome. Just looking at him made her stomach feel as squishy as a bowlful of meal worms. No, she wasn't going to turn him back into a human yet.

"Let's get going," Amber urged. "Every moment we waste is a moment that another mouse might get fed to a snake."

She led the way east, forging through tall grass.

Ben followed, seething. Soon they reached a place that he called "the millpond," where huge logs floated in dark-stained water, and cattail rushes grew all around. Just beyond it was a sawmill where gray smoke issued from a tall smokestack.

The millpond was vast, and traveling around it would have taken hours, so Ben suggested that they use the logs in the pond as a bridge, dashing across. As the mice drew near the water, Amber saw a muskrat swimming silently, gathering grasses from the bank to take to her young. In the deep rushes, a mother mallard duck sat on her nest. She looked at the mice and quacked softly, warning her ducklings, "Be careful, those mice can bite."

Then the mice reached the nearest log. These were huge Douglas fir trees, cut into long sections and left in the water to cure. Walking across one would be like walking across a bridge.

Ben took a couple of bounds and leaped onto the log. But Amber and Bushmaster had to climb up a prickly blackberry vine and use it as a rope bridge to reach the log.

Once they got a firm footing on the bark, they began scampering along. Amber peered into the dark water. The top of the pond held hundreds of water striders. They danced about, buoyed only by surface tension. Under the water, Amber saw snails clinging to the log, and a crayfish and guppies darting about in the shallows. Farther out, the pond seemed to be bottomless. This was the first time that Amber had ever seen deep water.

They reached the end of the log, and Ben easily leaped across to the next one. Bushmaster jumped too and narrowly reached it, but when Amber tried to make the long jump, she hit the water with a splash.

The millpond was cold and deep.

Frantically, she tried running to the log as fast as she could, but her feet couldn't get any purchase in the water, and she went under for a moment. She arched her back, raising her snout above the water line, and found herself swimming.

Ben shouted, "Just climb up the log."

Amber tried to grab the wood with her tiny nails, but the water weighed her fur down. So she slogged, treading water, desperately looking for a way up. There was no way that she could climb the sheer end of the log. She turned and saw huge lily pads floating in the shallows.

She tried to stop for a rest and bobbed under.

"Don't stop," Bushmaster shouted. "Swim for safety! You can do it."

But Amber was growing too tired to swim. She was just a pet shop mouse.

So she *wished* herself to the nearest lily pad and hurtled into the air like a cork popping from a bottle.

No sooner had she plopped onto the lily pad, still gasping and soggy, than an enormous fish exploded from the depths behind her. Its blood-red gills flashed in the sunlight, and crystalline drops of water scattered from it. Its tail churned mightily, lifting it far out of the pond.

"Got ya," the fish roared as it rose from the depths. Then, as it realized that it had missed, it muttered, "Never mind," and plopped back into the oily water.

"That's a bass!" Ben said, eyes wide with fright. "And he looks bigger than a killer whale!"

For a moment, Amber lay on the lily pad, realizing that she'd narrowly escaped death. She looked around. There were lots of lily pads in the shallows, enough so that she could use them like stepping stones. She'd have to follow the others.

Bushmaster looked up at the skies with distrust. Amber followed his gaze. Clouds had begun to gather—puffy and white on top, seething and gray at the bottom, filling the skies. Bushmaster whispered, "There's a hawk coming toward us. We've got to get under cover!"

Bushmaster took the lead, running and jumping between logs. Amber leaped from one lily pad to the next. When she reached the fourth lily pad, another bass sprung at her, crying, "Death from below!" It barely missed her.

"Watch out!" Ben cried. "This place is infested!"

Amber ran over the lily pads, back to the logs.

Bass were everywhere, surging from the water, driving from the depths. Twice more, Amber nearly got gobbled.

When the mice reached the far side of the pond, they hid, panting, among a forest of cattail rushes that rustled like paper in the wind. Overhead, the hawk finally came, but it did not spot them. They laughed in relief—all except for Ben, who had become sullen and thoughtful.

"We'd better be careful," Ben warned. "Those fish were just waiting for us. They knew that we were coming, and they only tried to eat Amber. It was a trap."

"What do you mean?" Bushmaster asked. "They couldn't have known we'd be here."

"I met a spider this morning," Ben confessed, looking away, "and he warned me that we are heading into danger. Most of the spiders have bet that we never even make it out of the pet shop alive."

Bushmaster asked, "What do the spiders know that we don't?"

"Amber has enemies," Ben said.

"No, I don't!" Amber objected. "Except for those snotty spotted mice at the pet shop, I don't have an enemy in the world."

"You're a wizardess," Ben said. "And other sorcerers want you dead." He looked as if he would say more, but he fell silent.

Amber trembled in fear. Old Barley Beard had warned her that whenever a person gained a little power, others would always try to pull her down. But who were her enemies? Who could marshal hawks and fish against her? And what dangers lay ahead?

Bushmaster said, "From now on, we'd better be extra careful."

"What else did the spider tell you?" Amber asked Ben. She needed to know more.

"Nothing," Ben said, looking away.

Amber was only ten weeks old, and she didn't know much, but she knew that Ben was lying. He'd learned something important, but he didn't want to tell her.

He doesn't love me, Amber realized. *That part of my dream wasn't true. And I guess he has a right to hate me, with the way I've been treating him.*

Amber felt bad. She could force the truth out of Ben, she knew, like she had done last night. He'd make more sickening gagging sounds as she tore the words from him.

But she didn't want to put him through that again.

"All right," she said. "You can keep your little secret if you want to. I just hope you know, Ben, that I'm not your enemy."

"I know," Ben said with hurt in his voice. "And I don't want to be your enemy either."

Amber let out a sigh of relief. Maybe there was some truth in her dream. She almost hoped that they could become friends.

So they forged through the tall grass as a storm gathered overhead. Hop, stop, and look, six eyes peering warily. With every step, Amber tried to be as quiet as a rock.

Amber whirled about, slurping them down like dust bunnies, firing them across the room like spit wads.

CHAPTER 10

THE BATTLE AT NOAH'S ARK

It isn't about how big the mouse is who is in the fight, it's about how big the fight is in the mouse.
—Doonbarra the Sugar Glider

At dusk, Ben led Amber and Bushmaster to the outskirts of town. Never before had the town seemed so strange and ominous, with its smelly cars growling like bears as they hunted along the bleak asphalt streets and houses looming above him like storybook giants.

Clouds now blackened the sky, a storm threatening. Ben's fears had been growing all day. Now, every nerve seemed electrified. His fur stood on end.

Ahead, Ben could see Noah's Ark in the shadows. Its outside was painted with kittens and puppies, which didn't look as innocent now as they had a couple of days ago.

Ben gripped his spear tightly. "Let's get this over with," he said as he led Amber and Bushmaster forward.

* * *

Inside the pet shop, the monster in the back room lurched to its feet. It climbed up on its back legs, peering around, all three eyes peering in different directions.

The monster had keen sight, keen ears, and a cunning mind. Now it went to work.

It grabbed the bars of its cage with its tentacles, squeezed its stomach hard, and slowly vomited out the contents.

What came out was no cute kitten. It was a large creature with blood-red hair covered in mucus, enormous ears, bits of wing as limp as rubber, and clawed feet.

Nightwing tumbled to the bottom of the cage, then struggled to his feet, gasping, and began to fan himself with his wings, trying to dry the mucus. He hissed to the monster, "Excellent, my friend. Now I know how Jonah felt inside the whale."

The monster was much thinner now, almost weasely.

"I not friend," the monster groaned, a sound like boulders rumbling together. "Freeee meeee."

"All in good time," Nightwing assured him. "First, you must kill the young wizardess. Bring me her corpse, and then I will free you."

The monster blinked all three eyes at once, a sign that it understood.

"But remember. Do not harm her familiar, the jumping mouse, Ben. He will be of more value to me alive."

The monster grunted in understanding. With that, it vaulted to the top of its cage, a jump of three feet straight up. Worming its tentacles between the bars, it grabbed several at once. With a vicious jerk, it pulled the bars wide, making a hole wide enough for a cannonball to fly through.

It jumped through, plopped to the floor, and wiggled forward on its tentacles, studying the room as if seeking a place to set an ambush.

Darwin pulled his proboscis from Nightwing's back and said, "Why do you want Ben alive? Wouldn't it be easier to kill him? I mean, if you cut the wizardess off from her source of power, she'll be easy to kill."

Nightwing grinned evilly. "Never mind. Don't tax your brain. You're not used to thinking."

"I do too think!" Darwin said. "I had an idea just last month."

"Really?" Nightwing asked. "Tell me about it."

Darwin stammered, scratched his tiny head with two of his feet, and said, "I was thinking that television is the new obsession of the masses."

"Interesting," Nightwing said. "You have a shallow mind, but it does have some deep spots. Sort of like sinkholes." Nightwing suspected that Darwin was lying, of course. He hadn't really come up with that idea on his own. He'd probably just eavesdropped on the beetles that lived on the floor of the cave. They often spouted such nonsense.

So Nightwing decided to test him. "Are you sure that *television* is the new obsession of the masses? Perhaps a decade ago, I'd have agreed. But lately it seems that the masses have begun to splinter—video games, consumerism, Ben and Jerry's ice cream, working out."

Darwin sat sucking blood with loud squishing sounds.

"So," Nightwing asked. "The real question is, Why does mankind seek an obsession in the first place? Are sunrises so miserable that they must escape from them? Or is it that they just have some innate longing for something better, for . . . perfection," Nightwing loved to infuriate the tick, so he added, "perhaps even a *spiritual* longing."

"Oh, no," Darwin growled. "Don't go there! I won't have any talk of 'spiritual longings.' We're all animals, not spiritual creatures. We're nothing more than a few basic elements combined in such a way so that we can amble about and stuff our guts. We're all just chemical accidents, and every child that is born is only a part of a runaway chain reaction. Someday, when the chain reaction reaches its end, we'll all just blow up!"

The tick went back to sucking blood in a rather morose fashion, but Nightwing smiled inwardly. At least Darwin had forgotten his original question—why Nightwing wanted Ben alive. The answer was simple. If Nightwing were to gain

Ben's power, the very foundations of the earth would tremble at his command.

If Nightwing could just let Ben see that Amber wasn't the kind of master that he should be serving, Nightwing could convince Ben to become *his* familiar.

Then Nightwing would finally be able to dispose himself of Darwin.

Nightwing chuckled as he flew up out of the cage and found a corner to hide in. He could hardly wait for Amber.

* * *

The lights were off at Noah's Ark Pet Shop, and the parking spaces empty. Ben heard the growl of distant thunder. He whispered to the others, "Let's get under a roof quickly, in case it starts to rain."

Ben raced to the front door of the pet shop, looking for a way in. But the crack under the door was too small, even for a mouse. So he led Amber to the back.

Several doors stood in a long row. Ben couldn't be sure which one led into the pet shop. He made a guess and went to a door that had a tiny hole under it where some mouse had chewed its way through long, long ago.

Ben took one last look outside. It was getting dark fast. He could see streetlights beginning to flick on. He sniffed the air. No sign of danger. But he smelled the rising storm. Ben worried about what might be inside, what trap any sorcerers might have set. The spider's warning wasn't something he'd taken lightly. His heart was racing.

But even more worrisome than the spider was the bat's warning: every time Amber cast a spell, she drained mage dust from Ben. And if she cast too many spells, she'd empty him out and never have enough to turn him back into a human. He had to stop her from using magic.

Taking a deep breath, he crawled under the door and peered in. Everything was dark. Gurgling sounds from the aquariums assured Ben that he was indeed inside the pet shop. Up a dark corridor, Ben could make out weird lights—heat lamps for terrariums and aquariums.

As soon as Amber and Bushmaster crawled in, Ben whispered, "This way!"

He began creeping up the corridor. Strange shapes huddled on both sides of him. He suspected that they were bags of dog food or boxes filled with birdseed, but in fact, he could hardly see a thing and couldn't be sure.

He neared the first terrarium, saw a huge anaconda large enough to swallow a small pig. The snake flicked its tongue. A loud hiss issued from its cage, echoing through the room. A command. "SSSS. SSSSS. SSSlither hither."

Ben glanced into the snake's haunting eyes. He felt compelled to move toward the cage and stumbled a bit, but Bushmaster nuzzled his shoulder, urging him forward and out of the trance.

Ben glanced back at Bushmaster. "Thanks," he said.

Ben and the others raced past the snake's cage and past a huge tank of gurgling water. Other terrariums held creatures that remained mostly unseen, hidden in shadows—lizards as big as dinosaurs, tarantulas as large as cars.

Ben raced past them, too afraid to look, and found a door cracked open, leading into the pet shop. Ben looked up. Above him now were the birds. Finches, mourning doves, and brightly colored macaws slept in their cages, eyes closed as they clung to their roosts. The massive birds looked like pterodactyls. He could almost picture the huge flying dinosaurs sitting high up on craggy cliffs as they silently watched for prey.

The only sounds came from the gurgling of water pumps in the fish tanks and the sweet music of crickets at the front of the store.

But the odor of animals was everywhere, the hair of dogs, the droppings of birds and guinea pigs.

Somewhere, a kitten began meowing, and Ben heard a banging noise on the far side of the store, as if a ferret were leaping about in its cage.

Ben hurried down an aisle and twisted to the right, where the aquariums were. The neon lights on the saltwater fish tanks glowed in the darkness, giving the room a strange ambience. Sea horses and eels clung to sea grass, hiding, while colorful reef fish darted about like living gems.

Ben heard a strange noise and looked up. Near the top of one tank, a light-tan octopus with blue rings splotched on its skin was staring at him with knowing eyes.

It sang in a strange voice, like metal warping under pressure far in the distance, "What is your song, child? What is your song?"

It was strangely similar to the question that Vervane had asked. Who are you? What is your song?

Ben felt empty. He had no song for the octopus. "I'm just a boy," he answered.

"Are you sure?" the octopus asked. "Or could you be something more?"

Amber and Bushmaster raced up behind him. Ben scrambled around a corner, threading past displays of sunken ships and twisted lumps of coral rock for aquariums.

The mouse cages were around the corner. Ben and his companions crept toward them, and suddenly something came plummeting out of the darkness.

It hit all three of them like a falling rhino.

Ben rolled to his side, trying to get under the lip of one of the display cases for safety. He gasped for breath, the wind knocked out of him, and faded from consciousness for a second. He heard shouts above, the voices of dozens of mice calling, "Watch out! There's a kitten loose!"

Cries of horror came from the mouse habitats, as if the mice were burning.

Ben peered up and dimly saw a tan-colored Abyssinian kitten with almond-shaped eyes and large ears. It was muscular, lithe, and evil looking all at once as it sat under the garish light of the fish tanks. It held Amber under its paw. She had been knocked senseless.

Bushmaster raced off into the darkness, shouting, "Run! Run!"

The kitten seemed gigantic. Ben had seen a lion once at Wildlife Safari. The big cat had been chest-high to him. But this monster towered above the mice like the statue of the Sphinx in Egypt. Each paw was nearly half as long as a mouse, and the retractable claws that hooked into Amber's back were the size of scythes.

"Purrrfect, purrrfect little mouse," the Abyssinian murmured. "Sooo purrrrrrfect."

Amber lay trapped beneath the cat's glistening claws. The pet shop mice screamed and swooned in their cages.

Ben peered about weakly, wondering how a kitten had gotten loose in the pet shop.

The kitten wasn't trying to eat Amber, just torment her. Ben wanted to run, but he knew that if he left Amber in the kitten's paws, she'd be killed.

What would happen if she did die? he wondered. *Would I grow old and die as a mouse in six months?*

He had no choice. Ben grabbed his needle, propped it up as if it were a cane, and hobbled forward.

"What do you think you're doing?" Ben demanded.

The kitten chuckled low in her throat, and said, "Purrrfect. She'll make a purrrfect present for my master. Then he'll praise me and pet me—purrrrfectly."

Ben saw the kitten shift just a little, its muscles bunching, its long, black-tipped tail whipping about playfully. It was just waiting for Ben to try something. But Ben felt too woozy to take on the kitten.

The mice in the cages were all calling to Amber, trying to rouse her. But their voices were muted by distance and the thick wall of glass that surrounded them.

Amber lay unmoving.

"Hey," Ben said. "If you're planning to eat her, doesn't she deserve a last wish?"

The kitten's eyes shone like bright copper. "A wish?" the kitten said. "No last wishes for this one. I've been warned."

So, Ben realized, *someone* had *talked to the kitten. This was all part of some plot! But who was behind it?*

The kitten licked Amber's head with her huge, rasping tongue. The gesture seemed to rouse the mouse, who lifted her head groggily. Amber kept gasping for breath as she lay crushed beneath the cat's paw.

The mice in their cage redoubled their cries, shouting, "Help her," and "Amber, run."

Amber lurched, trying in her daze to bolt free, but the kitten instantly grabbed tighter with her claws. The kitten threateningly gaped her mouth. Her fangs were as long and as white as elephant tusks. She prepared to puncture a hole through Amber's skull.

"Wait!" Ben said as he gripped his makeshift spear and stalked closer to the giant kitten. "You were warned about Amber, but was your boss smart enough to warn you about me?"

The Abyssinian peered at Ben's weapon. She growled deep in her throat. "Stay back. You're one step away from mouse heaven."

The Abyssinian could squash him in an instant, Ben knew, but it held onto Amber and began backing away, dragging her along. It seemed to be frightened.

"Tell me who sent you," Ben demanded. "Or I swear, I'll stab you right in the eye!"

The Abyssinian stopped. At that instant, there was a piercing sound, and the kitten vaulted three feet in the air.

Bushmaster was behind the cat. He'd sneaked up on her and stabbed her tail.

The Abyssinian came down in a quivering heap.

Ben didn't even think about what he was doing. He leaped toward the creature with all his might, thrusting his spear deep into its shoulder, and Bushmaster did the same, stabbing the cat in the back.

The Abyssinian yowled, rolling backward. It scrabbled to its feet with its back arched, hair standing up along its spine.

Bushmaster squatted, his spear aimed threateningly at the cat, and Ben felt gratitude well up inside him. He was suddenly very thankful to know this vole, to have won his friendship.

"Beware," Ben shouted at the Abyssinian. "We mice have weapons now, and we're a match for any cat!"

The kitten hissed and sped around a corner.

Ben leaned on his spear and nodded at Bushmaster.

"Good job," Bushmaster said.

"Thank you for being here," Ben replied. Ben looked at Bushmaster, and for a tiny instant he thought of his old friend, Christian. Christian had been the kind of friend that you could count on in a crunch, just like Bushmaster, and he had the same kind of happy-go-lucky nature that the vole did when he broke into song.

For a moment, Ben realized how much the two were alike, and the moment melted into sadness.

"Hooray!" the feeder mice in their cage all shouted. They cheered in delight, and many of them trembled and wept in relief.

Amber moaned softly. Bushmaster crept forward and nuzzled her. Ben heard a chuckling sound and looked up. There was a huge cage there with black bars above him. Something like a wooden birdhouse was inside, with bits of rope, vine, and tree branches forming a false jungle. In the dim light provided by the fish tanks, Ben could barely make out a creature in the shadowy wood box.

"Good on ya, mates," a loud, deep voice said. "You put the fear o' mice into that one, all right!"

The creature inched forward and peered through the bars. It wasn't anywhere near as large as its voice made it sound. Its fur was brightly colored—bluish gray on the sides and back with a lighter gray stomach, black circles around its eyes and on its ears, and a black stripe blazing its forehead. It looked kind of like a chipmunk, except that its snout was too long, too pointy, and too pink.

"Hello," Ben said.

"G'day back on ya," the creature said. It studied him for a moment, as if content just to watch the show.

Ben didn't know what to do now. Amber was still unconscious, with Bushmaster nuzzling her. Just ahead stood a bench with the mouse cage on it.

"Watch out for that kitten, while I free the mice," Ben warned Bushmaster as he loped toward to the cage.

The bench was too high to reach, so he uncurled his fishing line, made some knots in it, and hurled the treble hook up into the air. It caught on the wooden bench, and Ben began to pull himself up.

It was hard work. His arms burned from the effort, but Ben told himself, "Come on, you wimp. You can do it! You couldn't weigh more than an ounce now."

In moments, he'd reached the top. There were twenty-four feeder mice in the cage where Ben had bought Amber. They were kept inside a terrarium that only had half of a lid covering it. The mice raced up to him and peered through the glass. They were all plain brown in color, and most of them looked young, only a few weeks old.

"Who are you?" they asked.

"Are you a wild mouse?"

"What are you doing with Amber?"

One plain brown feeder mouse maiden looked shyly at Ben, then begged, "Will you marry me?"

"I'm here to rescue you," Ben told them. "We're going to take you to the Endless Meadow."

"Hooray," the feeder mice cried. They began racing around their pen, leaping for joy.

Ben gathered his fishing line and threw the treble hook into the mouse's cage. It snagged on the food dish, and he pulled the line tight.

"Climb on out," he told them. In moments, the mice were clinging to the fishing line, climbing up four at a time. Ben held the line on his side, so that the feeder mice wouldn't pull it in.

When the first one reached safety, Ben ordered, "Help keep an eye out for that kitten." And he held on tight as the rest of the mice kept climbing.

Soon, mice were tumbling from the cage right and left.

Overhead, on a higher shelf, lived the spotted mice. They saw what was happening and left their exercise wheels and their gourmet mouse food to watch the show.

Once Ben had the feeder mice out of their cage, he worked his treble hook free from the water dish, and, with a bit of work, climbed now to the top shelf.

Ben threw a line to the spotted mice, but none of them went to it. One asked, "Why would we want to go with you? We have a fabulous home and tantalizing food. Besides, we don't want to be seen with *ugly* mice."

Some others shouted, "Yeah, we don't want to be seen with *yooo-eww*."

A feeder mouse shouted back, "Yeah, well you smell poopy!"

"You're just jealous," a spotted mouse said, "because we're better than you."

From the floor, Amber said reasonably, "You *are* prettier than us. But all mice are beautiful. The humans might not see that, but we mice should see the truth."

Ben looked down. Amber had regained her feet. She sounded wise and reasonable and much more mature than her ten weeks. She was gazing up at Ben with tears of gratitude in her eyes. The feeder mice were leaping from the table, gathering around her. She rejoiced to see her friends.

Ben felt proud to have saved the mice and even prouder that he had done it all on his own.

"Yeah, well you're ugly," one spotted mouse shouted at Amber. "And if you can't see that, then maybe you're more than ugly. Maybe you're stupid, too!"

The spotted mice reminded Ben of some kids he knew at school. They never had a nice word for anyone but themselves.

Ben wanted to save the spotted mice, but he knew that he couldn't force them to come against their will. He offered a warning. "I have news for you. Brown mice are raised to be food for snakes and lizards, and so we needed to free them. But if you stay here, the humans will need to feed the snakes something, and it just might be you."

One spotted mouse smiled condescendingly, as if Ben were a fool. "The humans would never hurt me." She twirled, displaying her lovely brown coat with white spots. "I'm too beautiful. And pretty mice are far too valuable to be put on the menu."

"Well," Ben said, as he pulled his fishing line back to himself and coiled it, "If I were a snake, I think I'd much rather eat a pretty mouse than a plain old brown one."

He watched the spotted mice, to see if any would come, but they all began running on their exercise wheel, munching on mouse yogurt bars, or drinking Evian from their water spigot. None of them would come. Ben said, "Have a nice life," and turned away.

But as he looked down the aisle from his high vantage point, he spotted a calico kitten crouching atop a fish tank at the far end of turtle aisle, waiting to pounce on any mice that might be traveling unaware.

At that moment all of the mice were just in front of him on the floor below. Ben spotted movement farther off—several kittens on the next aisle, sneaking on all fours.

In a mighty leap, Ben jumped to the ground and rushed up to Amber. She stood at the center of a knot of mice that had gathered around her and Bushmaster with their tails pointing out. Most of them were squealing with delight, greeting Amber as if she'd been gone for years.

"Amber," Ben shouted. "Your friends are free. Now turn me back into a human. Quick!"

Startled, Amber looked at Ben. She'd been smiling, but now her face fell. Ben could see hesitation in her dark eyes. Maybe even fear.

She doesn't want to turn me back, he realized. "Hurry," Ben urged. "The kittens are coming!"

Amber whirled to look down the aisle, and sure enough, just then the Abyssinian stepped into their field of view. Behind it came others—a black Persian with orange eyes whose hair was so thick it looked like armor and a pair of yellow-striped, tigerlike kittens.

The Abyssinian roared. "You think you're so tough. Let's see how you handle a pride of us."

Amber looked back at Ben and said, "I wish . . . I wish . . ." Amber's heart pounded like a cricket in her chest. She licked her lips and peered about in terror. Ben could almost read her mind, trying to find a reason, any reason, not to keep her part of the bargain.

Was it because she really didn't want to lose him? Or was there something more? Maybe she had guessed the truth, that *he* was the source of her power.

The kittens saw Amber's fear and took courage. There was a sea of them, and they stalked forward quietly, like a fog that rolls along the ground, their tails twitching menacingly in the sky. Ben could hear their evil, hissing laughter.

Amber peered back at Ben, weighing her choices, and roared, "I wish that I were a giant, cat-sucking vacuum cleaner!"

Blue lights flashed, piercing her skin, and bolts of lightning went zapping overhead, frying holes in the ceiling and exploding into walls.

Amber growled and her face twisted into something hideous. Bits of metal began piercing through her hair, as if nails were trying to poke through her. Suddenly she rose up in the air, high above the rest of the mice. Her gray mouse hairs formed into huge needles, like spear points sticking out from her body. Her feet and paws became terrifying metal talons. Her chest and stomach turned to clear plastic, and all of her intestines looked like coils of glass tubes. Her long snout became a huge silver cannon, and her belly issued a terrible rumbling sound, as if she were a cement truck.

But the worst thing was her eyes. Her eyes grew huge and blazed like a furnace of green fire.

The mice around her all shrieked and fled, running for cover. Amber was a giant now—a clumsy giant—as dangerous as any cat. She grabbed for something to hang onto, and one huge arm slapped the black cage above Ben, knocking it to the floor. Its door flung open, and the chipmunklike creature scrambled for cover.

The Abyssinian watched Amber's transformation in awe, its back arching. "You don't scare us," it hissed.

Amber charged down the aisle, past angelfish that gaped in dismay. After two steps she took one huge leap and landed on iron feet among the kittens.

Sluuurrrppp! She sucked the Abyssinian up in one second, and the next moment Ben could see the terrified kitten tumbling through her innards, twisting, turning, and clawing, desperately grasping at the glass walls, its mouth wide in terror.

The Abyssinian hit Amber's stomach with a thunking sound and whirled around the vacuum chamber, bouncing and rattling against the walls, yowling in terror.

Just then, Amber raised her long tail, now covered in silver barbs, as if it were a glittering, deadly hose. She aimed it over the nearest aisle, and the Abyssinian went roaring through it, whooshed over the fish tanks, and landed in a mound of twitching fur.

It just lay on its back, petrified with fear, its claws grabbing the air, eyes staring into oblivion.

The other kittens had all arched their backs and were hissing in terror, sidestepping but too afraid to run.

Amber charged in among the kittens. They yowled in terror. They clawed and cursed as only evil kittens can. They ran, scrambling under fish tanks and over shelves—but it did them no good.

Amber whirled about, slurping them down like dust bunnies, firing them across the room like spit wads.

Ben watched in terror—not terror at Amber's power, but at the waste of it.

She was using all of the magic he kept stored inside.

The mice cheered as Amber chugged kittens. "Yay," they all shouted. "Think twice before you mess with mice!"

It was a great victory for Amber and a terrible defeat for Ben.

The chipmunklike creature hopped up to Ben and asked in a deep voice, “Why so glum, mate?”

“She didn’t turn me back into a human,” Ben said bitterly. “She didn’t keep her promise. And I don’t think that she ever will.”

At the far end of the hallway near the door, something dark and sickening slogged into view.

CHAPTER II

THE DARK MAGE

There's a little monster in everyone.
—NIGHTWING

AMBER RACED through the pet shop, chasing kittens, swallowing them whole, and shooting them out. Her thoughts swam in a red river of rage. She kept remembering how the Abyssinian had enjoyed tormenting her. She recalled the little song that Domino had sung about nibbling the heads off of mice, and she understood something that she'd never imagined. For a cat, killing was play.

How many mice had died beneath cats' paws? How old was time? How wide was the world? And in that ageless, vast world, how many mice had died in torment?

"Stop it," Amber shouted through a red haze of rage. "Stop killing us. Stop it now!"

Everything became a blur. Amber chased evil kittens through the pet shop, past aisles brimming with puppy chew toys, around a koi pond where fountains burbled and enormous fish swam lazily beneath the lily pads, and over the tops of lizard cages where iguanas and bearded dragons lazed beneath artificial suns.

In her haste to grab one white kitten, she ripped open a huge bag of fish food. Dried flies and brine shrimp whooshed through her belly and shot out her tail, then sat glittering in the air. A Siamese kitten tried to climb over a birdcage and knocked it to the floor. Amber lunged through displays of dog collars to reach it.

Around the room, Amber chased the kittens, finding them hiding behind cans of dog food and climbing under counters. She tore the pet shop apart, smashing cages and hurling bags of birdseed, all in her effort to find them.

She saw a huge kitten on a nearby wall, ran to it, and attacked it with her claws. The kitten shredded, and Amber saw that it was just a picture. Just a picture.

Behind the picture, the wall was made of cinder blocks. Amber's metal claws had gouged a trail.

She stared at it in shock. Distantly she heard a small voice. "Amber, stop! Stop!"

Numb, she turned and looked down. Ben and Bushmaster were on the floor nearby. Both held their spears, and Ben wore his silly little helmet made of walnut shell. Bushmaster stared at her in fear and surprise.

"Stop it," Ben shouted. "The kittens are gone. They've all gone back to their cage."

Amber turned. The terrified kittens were indeed back in their cage, shivering in fear. Amber hadn't meant to hurt them, but she saw cats limping about, one with a torn ear, some with swollen eyes.

Indeed, everywhere that she looked, the animals were cowering in terror. A tank full of turtles looked like nothing but turtle shells. Snakes were burrowing holes in the sands of their cages. Cockatoos cowered in the shadows.

Amber's heart pounded so hard, it was as if there was a hammer inside, beating to get out.

I'm as tall as a human, she thought. *Everything is smaller than me. Nothing can hurt me.*

For the first time in her life, Amber realized what it was to be free—free from the fear of being eaten, free to move across the world at will.

What a wonderful thing it must be to be human, she thought. *Free from all cages. Free to grow old.*

Yet she looked down at Ben and saw how handsome he was. Strong and sleek and precious.

"I wish," she said. "I wish I were a mouse again."

And she shrank. Her metal claws became flesh. The clear plastic lining of her stomach grew fur. In seconds, she was a mouse, wrung out and tired, panting on the floor.

Ben and Bushmaster came up to her. Amber asked, "Where did everyone else go?"

"They're hiding," Ben said. "They were afraid."

From down here, Amber could understand why. Cans of animal food were strewn all across the floor. Ripped bags and broken bottles.

"This way," Ben said. He led her down the aisle and around the corner to the fish section. Amber saw the destruction she'd wrought. One fish tank was cracked, water leaking everywhere. Bright parrotfish were flopping about in the white sand.

"I wish that tank were full of water," Amber said. Immediately, water whisked up from the floor, filling the tank. With a thought Amber resealed the tank, as good as new.

The bottom shelves on this aisle were filled with ceramic statues—sunken warships full of holes where guppies and swordtails could dart among the ruins, pirate skulls where eels could live among the eye sockets while bottom-feeders cleaned the teeth, haunted houses where the souls of dead ghost crabs might linger for decades.

Ben led Amber into the hollow of a treasure chest where gold coins seemed to spill out of an old wooden box bound with iron rings. Ben nuzzled the lid open. The pet shop mice huddled inside, trembling.

They looked at Amber, and their fear worsened. "Don't hurt us," one mouse pup cried. "Please!"

Amber realized that she wasn't the mouse that had grown up in their cage anymore. They didn't look at her and see their savior. She was a monster.

"I'm sorry," Amber said. "I won't hurt you. I would never hurt you."

Amber looked up at all of the damage that she had done and imagined that she would repair it. She'd restore the ripped bags of animal food and remove the dent from every can.

"Don't try to fix everything," Ben said, as if reading her mind. "Save your magic."

Something in Ben's tone made her worry. "What do you mean, save my magic?"

"Don't you know?" Ben said. "It runs out!"

"Runs out?"

Ben tried to explain. "Like the food in your feeding cup," Ben said. "Each time you eat a little, the food drops lower, until there is none left at all."

"Oh," Amber said, suddenly understanding. She had felt so powerful and dangerous a moment ago. Now she only felt bewildered.

"And think," Ben said. "You have powerful sorcerers out to get you, but all they've done is send a few cuddly kittens to kill us. Your enemies are just trying to wear you down. I don't think that the real fight has even started."

He gave her a warning look, and Amber realized that he could be right. Perhaps they were still in danger.

"Let's go," Ben told the other mice. "Hop, stop, and look. Hop, stop, and look."

The mice climbed out of the treasure chest, flowing over the gold coins. They followed Ben's lead, timidly making their way across the floor.

The room was filled with shadows. Nothing moved in the shadows, but as Amber neared the end of the aisle, she heard a thumping of feet. Once, twice, three times the sound of footsteps pounded on the plastic hood of a fish tank. She whirled to look behind her and saw a shadowy form leap across one aisle to the next.

It happened so fast, she almost thought that she imagined it. But then the creature landed among a stack of cans with a clank and disappeared into the shadows.

"What was that?" the mice cried.

Amber could see nothing. Still, she knew that they were being followed.

At the end of the aisle, they turned and headed warily for the back door. Hop, stop, and look. Hop, stop, and look. The feeder crickets at the front counter had nearly all gone silent. Only a lone cricket sang in the darkness. A terrarium on the counter had some sickly green vines twisting in it. Amber saw something move inside, and three mice cried out at once.

It was a horned chameleon, as green as the vines it hid among. Only its strange little eye had moved.

Amber took some comfort in knowing that there wasn't much that could hide from twenty-seven frightened mice.

Ben called the mice to a halt and whispered, "Keep low under the lip of the counter here. Follow me in single file. Try not to be seen. Amber, I'll take the front. You guard the rear."

Ben led them to the storeroom door and crept under it. Inside the backroom, he darted behind a stand that held a terrarium and crept in the narrow space between it and the wall. The space was about half an inch wide—just narrow enough for a mouse to squeeze through. That gave Amber a sense of comfort. No large animals could follow them.

They crept that way for half the length of the hallway, sneaking beneath a terrarium filled with giant komodo dragons sleeping beneath their blue lights and past another tank where giant snakes hissed in their sleep.

Amber heard the thump of feet behind her. She glanced back and saw a shadow slip under the door and race into the room. Whatever creature was following them, it was much larger than a mouse—both longer and taller.

It ran past the crack that the mice traveled through and disappeared into the room.

Good, it's lost our trail, she thought.

She inched forward.

Ben had reached a spot where a huge fish tank pressed solidly against the wall. A bunch of cords ran from wall plugs up into the tank, then disappeared down into a box that burbled and made bubbles in the thick, algae-clouded water.

Ben raced to the nearest electrical cord, set his spear between his teeth, leaped up, and began to climb. When he reached the top of the fish tank, he took his spear in hand and stood guard while the other mice followed.

Amber waited her turn. She fit her paws around the heavy rubber cord and climbed it as if it were a vine. When she got high enough, she could see into the tank. Huge fish swam inside, ugly fish with fangs as sharp as anything she'd seen on kittens. They swam in their tank, then lunged against the glass, trying to get to her.

She reached the top and found that most of the tank was open on top. The mice were running across a narrow bridge made of wood.

Amber was halfway across, when she sensed something. There was danger ahead. She couldn't see it, couldn't smell it or hear it. Yet she felt certain that death waited for her.

"Stop," she called to the mice.

The mice ahead all came to a halt and looked back at her. A hush fell across the room, and the sense of foreboding deepened.

Suddenly, at the far end of the hallway near the door, something dark and sickening slogged into view. It was like an octopus dragging a giant dead rat. But it gazed about, and Amber saw that the rat was alive, horribly alive. The monster was hunting.

It stopped in the middle of the floor and peered into the shadows with three angry eyes, eyes so full of pain that they seemed like coals. Hiding in the shadows as Amber was, the creature couldn't see her. It was blinded by the lights from the fish tank.

The creature waved its tentacles in a mystic gesture, and the air around the creature darkened, turning to shadows so that it faded from view, obscured by a mist.

The mist flowed away from Amber and lodged into a corner between some bags of birdseed until it looked like just another shadow.

Every nerve in Amber's brain screamed a warning. This creature wasn't natural. And it was hunting her.

Silently, she crept forward, following Ben and the other mice.

Soon they were hidden behind boxes again, tracing the wall to the door.

Ben darted out, dove beneath the hole in the door, and went outside. As soon as he was out, Bushmaster followed. Up ahead of her in the line, a mouse whispered, "Everybody sneak out, one at a time."

A third mouse scurried to safety, and a fourth, but each time that a mouse ran for cover, the next mouse waited less time before running for the hole, and soon they were pushing and shoving, trying to get outside.

Amber stayed hidden, glancing down the hallway.

A shadow separated from the pet foods, and flowed toward the fleeing mice. Within that shadow, Amber could discern movement. Tentacles waved hypnotically, and blue lights flashed in the mist. She heard a deep voice whisper, weaving some fearsome spell.

Suddenly, a glob of slobber hurtled out of the mist, thundering toward the fleeing mice. It arced through the air, and at the last instant fanned out into what looked like a huge spiderweb made of green snot.

It slammed into the mice, pinning them to the ground. They struggled against the ooze, but to no avail. The slightest touch held them.

And now the monster reached out with one tentacle and grabbed a long green line of goo. It began grunting as it pulled the web, dragging the mice toward it.

Amber stepped from the shadows and shouted, "I wish—" just as a second wall of snot flew into her.

The stuff hit her like a brick, knocking her back and leaving her dazed. She found herself pinned against the wall, green goop gluing her in place.

The stuff was so sticky that she couldn't move a muscle, couldn't even open her mouth.

Through a gap, she eyed the shadow. Now it evaporated like a mist, and the monster rose up on it hind legs. "I am the mighty Ratzilla," it cried. "The time for your unmaking is here."

It waved its tentacles, and a bolt of blue light shot toward Amber.

A thought flashed through her head, a longing to be outside, away from this mess.

Suddenly, there was a whoosh of air and a pop, and Amber found herself and all of the other pet shop mice rolling on the cement driveway outside.

She slammed into a dandelion, and white dandelion down floated all around her.

There was a whoosh, a mighty explosion. Fire and smoke issued from the back of the pet shop, and the door blew across the little parking lot.

Ratzilla stalked through the smoke, cruel and unstoppable.

He peered at all of the pet shop mice, his horrible eyes looking three directions at once. But it was very hard to see through all of those tentacles waving around its mouth. "Come," the creature shouted. "You cannot escape me!"

Amber saw Ben and a pair of pet shop mice crouching by the wall, just beside where the door had been. Ben grasped his spear and hopped toward the monster in a mighty leap, but Ratzilla whirled, caught Ben in all eight tentacles, and hurled him thirty feet through the air.

"Help!" Ben called.

"Leave us alone," Amber cried. And suddenly Ratzilla went hurtling through the air, blasting up like a firework and shooting into the stratosphere in a gorgeous display of scintillating purple sparks.

Amber had no idea where he went. She looked up, and he was just flying, flying, up toward the black clouds.

"And I wish you'd stay gone forever," she added.

Suddenly there was a flash as three bolts of lightning struck from three separate points on the horizon, streaking all across the sky to converge on the purple lights. For a moment, Amber went blind from the display, and then the heavens grumbled, growling with displeasure.

Ben plopped on the ground beside Amber and shook the stars out of his head. All of the mice began to cheer, and they converged on Amber, shouting, "Amber the Cat Killer. Amber the Brave!"

Their voices were a distant roaring in her ears. Amber peered up at the sky, and her eyes filled with tears. Her heart was nearly breaking.

"It's time," she told Ben. "It's time for me to turn you back into a human."

Ben looked up at her in surprise, unable to find his voice.

"But—" he began to say.

"No buts," Amber said, her decision final. "You've kept your part of the bargain and did it heroically. You helped free the mice of the world, and now its time to receive your reward."

"But, I didn't," Ben said. "I can't tell a lie. I *didn't* keep my part of the bargain."

Amber looked at him, unsure of what she was hearing. "What do you mean you didn't keep your part of the bargain?"

"I mean that I didn't help free the mice of the world," Ben said. "I helped free the mice from your pet shop, but that's just one pet shop. There are thousands and thousands of pet shops in the world, with millions of mice in them that still need to be freed! Even if we found a pet shop a day and freed all of the mice in it, we'd never get the job done. I've been thinking. You mice breed so fast, that no matter what we do, more mice will be born to cages than we can possibly free!"

Amber's mind did a little flip. She thought about that. *How big is the world?* she wondered. She really had no idea. Ben was telling her that it was far more vast than she had ever imagined. Could anyone possibly free all of the mice in it, unlock all of the cages?

And why was Ben telling her this? Then she understood. "Thank you, Ben, for being honest. That's noble of you. It's easy to be honest when there is nothing at stake, but it's far more difficult to tell the truth when it could cost you dearly. Nevertheless, we made a deal. In my mind, I wanted your help in freeing the mice from the pet shop where I was born—nothing more. And so I free you."

Amber raised her paws in a magical gesture that just felt natural and was about to turn Ben back into a human when he stopped her. "Wait!" he said. "I want to say good-bye to Bushmaster."

He turned to look through the crowd of mice that surrounded him and Amber. "Bushmaster," he called. "Bushmaster?"

But the vole was nowhere in sight.

Ben hopped away from the group, worry suddenly growing in his voice. Amber recalled the strange creature that had been following her through the pet shop. A kitten? A ferret?

"Bushmaster, where are you?" She wished that she could see him, and suddenly the door that had blown off of the pet shop earlier erupted into the air, flying hundreds of feet, then fluttered back to earth like a leaf blowing in a strong wind.

Beneath it lay Bushmaster, crushed. "Help!" Ben called, rushing to the vole. Amber was right behind him, hopping over weeds in the parking lot. There was little light in the sky, only the dim lights thrown by a single streetlamp. So it wasn't until Amber drew close that she could see how badly Bushmaster was hurt. Dark blood pooled from his nose and ears, and Bushmaster was trembling, his tiny feet and paws kicking uselessly. His eyes stared upward, but he seemed to see nothing.

"He's dying," Ben cried. He turned to Amber, huge tears welling up in his eyes. "Save him."

But Amber looked at the vole, and she knew that it was useless. Bushmaster wasn't dying, he was already dead. He must have been behind the door when Ratzilla blew it off of its hinges.

"He's already gone, I think," Amber said.

"Then bring him back," Ben said. "Bring him back from the dead."

The very thought startled Amber. Could she really do that with her powers? How vast were they?

"I wish I knew if he were alive," Amber said.

Suddenly, she could hear the little vole's heart beating in a flurry, but slowing. And she could see into him, as if his body were made of glass. And there at the center, deep, deep inside, she saw light—a tiny ember—throbbing and struggling to stay lit.

"Please," Ben said. "Heal him now. Even if it takes all of your power. Just do it!"

Amber looked up at Ben and realized the sacrifice he was offering to make, and her heart nearly broke at the thought. A noble mouse indeed!

And Amber shouted, "Bushmaster the vole, I wish that you were alive and well."

Bushmaster kicked his feet wildly, and Amber could see the tiny light in him, ready to go out. The vole twisted his head to the side, and there was a cracking noise. His skull, which had seemed a bit lopsided, popped back into shape. There was movement beneath him, and the fur at his belly suddenly seemed to zip closed.

He kept kicking, moaning in pain, and then suddenly leaped onto his feet and looked around groggily. His eyes brightened, and Amber could see into him perfectly. He flashed inside, and became a living light.

"I saw Him!" Bushmaster cried. "I saw Him! In the Endless Meadow!"

"Saw who?" Ben asked.

"The Great Master of Field and Fen, the Maker."

He suddenly spun toward Ben. "You should have seen it. There was darkness and a mist and a hole that led toward a great light. And when I got there, I saw wild peas growing in a riot and sunflowers as tall as trees and fields that smelled so sweet that you wanted to even eat the dirt. And there were no hawks in the sky or weasels in the holes. I saw mice and voles rushing about, playing in the open, totally free of fear. And then He came to me, in a great light, and . . . and . . ." Bushmaster turned to Ben and said, "and He told me, 'Your work is not yet finished. But be true and great shall be your reward.' And then I found myself being pulled backward, and I didn't want to leave, but before I knew it, I was back here."

Ben leaped forward, threw his arms around Bushmaster, and began to weep. "I'm so happy that you're alive," he said.

The mice all began to cheer again, leaping for joy, and Amber just watched them all sadly, letting Ben have a moment to say good-bye, until one of the younger female mice said. "Whew, I'm glad that's over. Now what is there to eat around here?"

With that, Amber suddenly realized that she was hungry too. It had been a long day, and she was ready for a bite of food and some sleep.

Ben looked around the weed-choked parking lot for something a mouse might eat. Then he seemed to get an idea and smiled over at the young girl. "You hungry?" he asked. "What's your favorite food?"

"Mouse pellets."

"We won't find any mouse pellets outside the pet shop. Is there anything that you don't like to eat?"

"Mouse pellets," the young girl said.

Ben looked at her strangely, and Amber said, "She's never eaten anything *but* mouse pellets."

"You should try some root mold," Bushmaster offered. "Now that's good eatin'!"

"What do you like?" the young girl asked. She was twisting side to side, and Amber suddenly realized that the girl had a crush on Ben. It was easy to see why. He was handsome, daring. He'd fought a cat and set her free. But the mouse, Peablossom was her name, was much too young for Ben.

"I like pizza," Ben said. "Ham with pineapple, and root beer to drink."

"Oh," Peablossom said in a daze. "Let's have that!"

Ben started to laugh and then looked over at Amber, as if asking permission.

It looked like a dragon, winging its way toward him, ghostly and purple.

CHAPTER 12

THE STORM

On some days, you can lick a gator;
on other days, the gator gobbles you for dinner.
—Rufus Flycatcher

BEN AND THE PET SHOP MICE celebrated their good fortune at Fat Jim's Pizza. It had been an easy matter for Ben to lead the mice there, only a couple of blocks from the pet shop, and then have Amber *wish* that the folks inside would deliver a few pizzas and some root beer. Fat Jim brought the food out himself in something of a daze. He bowed and scraped and presented the meal, thanking the mice profusely for their business, seemingly unaware that he was talking to rodents.

The pizzas were steaming hot, fresh from the oven. Ham and pineapple, pepperoni and cheese, one with everything, and one—specially ordered just for Bushmaster—was the Vegetarian's Ambrosia. The root beer had been delivered in huge glass goblets with plenty of straws and napkins.

The mice sniffed at the pizza, and Ben was satisfied to hear their little stomachs grumbling. Bushmaster gingerly crept up to the edge of his pizza, reached down with a paw, and scooped up a glob of mozzarella cheese. "Hey," he said with delight after downing a bite, "it's got *mold* in it!"

"Yeah," Ben said. "It's moldy milk. We humans call it cheese."

"Wow," Bushmaster cried. "This is really good!" Then he raced over the hot pizza on tiptoe, crying "Ouch, ooh, aah!" as he stepped, and began scooping up bits of artichoke heart, sun-dried tomato, mushrooms, and other delicacies.

Then the mice began scrambling all over the pizzas, while others were trying to get to the root beer. Amber wished a fork up against one of the goblets. It was great fun to watch Bushmaster climb to the edge, do a double somersault, belly flop into the goblet, and then sink to the bottom and peer out with big eyes like a goldfish before he climbed out. Soon, all of the mice were taking turns.

Ben filled himself up on ham and pineapple pizza. It was like heaven. His own pizza. It looked like it was as large as a flying saucer, and it was half as tall as him.

He was nibbling contentedly, watching the newly freed pet shop mice have the time of their lives, when Amber came over to him.

"Thank you," she said. "I owe you an apology."

"For what?" Ben asked.

"For thinking badly of you," Amber said. "I was afraid that you'd break our bargain, or run away. But more than that, I realize now that I should never have forced you to make a deal like that. It's not your fault that other humans imprison mice."

"Thank you," Ben said. "I'm sorry too, Amber. I shouldn't have tried to feed you to that lizard, no matter what my dad said."

Amber whispered, "That was a brave thing that you did, letting me heal Bushmaster."

"I had to," Ben said. "He's my friend."

"Are you always so good to your friends?" Amber said.

"I don't know," Ben said. "I don't have many. I used to have a friend, Christian. But he moved away." Ben found that his throat grew tight as he talked about Christian. He had never told anyone what he was about to tell Amber now. "His dad told me that he got a job at a penguin cannery in the Antarctic, and so they had to move. But I know that that's not true. Some kids at school said that they heard that Christian got sick and went into the hospital. He had cancer. I think that he died there, because if he was still alive, he would have sent me an e-mail, or called on the phone to talk, or—or—something."

Amber leaned forward, stroked Ben's fur with her paws. It was kind of nice, but Ben suddenly realized that he was being petted by a girl.

“What are you doing?” he asked, backing away.

“Preening you,” Amber said.

“What for?”

“It keeps the cooties off.”

“Oh,” Ben said. Then he let her preen him for a moment. He felt overwhelmed with sadness. He missed Christian.

Overhead, the heavens grumbled, and hail started to fall from the sky. It rained down, and the shiny pebbles, like boulders, bounced all over the pavement. The mice peered at the spectacle in awe as lightning flashed from hill to hill.

But the protective umbrellas at Fat Jim’s Pizza just shook in the high wind and let the hail bounce off. The mice were well protected. Only a few drops of hail bounced around on the table.

“Are you ready,” Amber asked, “to be human again?”

Ben nodded but added, “Amber, when you turn me back into a human, I don’t think I’ll be able to understand mouse talk anymore. But I want you to know that you’re welcome in my house anytime. In fact, I was thinking that maybe you and the other pet shop mice could come live in my backyard. That way, I could bring you food and stuff.”

Amber smiled gratefully, stopped her preening, and gave him a hug. “I’d like that,” she said. She seemed to think for a moment, and then she asked, “Ben, do you still think I’m ugly? Like a what-do-you-call-it, a parasitic worm?”

“No,” Ben said. “I think that you’re the prettiest mouse I’ve ever seen.”

Then, with her eyes full of tears, she said, "Ben Ravenspell, I wish that you were human again."

Ben felt the pain hit him as his bones began to grow under his skin. He suddenly ballooned to the size of a dog, and his tail felt as if it were being sucked up inside him. His nose was pulling in too, and he stared at his paw as it began to transform into a hand.

Then something strange happened. Amber cried in pain and staggered away from Ben, falling to the top of the table.

And Ben began to shrink back down to mouse size. Then he blew up again like a puffer fish, his tail growing back. It was as if his skin were bubbling tar, rising one moment, shrinking the next. One moment his hand was as big as a human's, but with every tiny hair and detail just like a mouse's; then the next he was shrinking down.

"What's wrong?" Ben cried. "Are you out of power?"

But when he looked at Amber, he saw that she was in no condition to answer. She was lying on the ground, apparently having fainted, tossing and turning and crying in pain.

"Amber," Ben cried, as he tried crawling toward her.

And suddenly he was a mouse, nothing more than a mouse. But Amber was still trembling, unconscious, and twisting in pain.

The heavens rumbled, as if with thunder, and Ben heard a single word. "Behold," the heavens said. Ben looked up. Lightning flashed across the sky, and far above, Ben saw a huge cloud light up. It looked like a dragon, winging its way toward him, ghostly and purple. "Behold your weakness!"

But as he peered up, he saw that it was no dragon. It was a bat, an enormous bat wide enough to swallow the world.

It roared as it dove toward him, and all of the pet shop mice screamed and leaped off of the table. Only Ben stood over the fallen Amber. He grabbed his spear and held steady.

But the mighty dragon shape began to diminish, growing smaller as it neared until finally the bat Nightwing plopped onto the table and stood over Amber's fallen body.

"Put that away," he said, with a wave of his clawlike wing, and Ben's spear went flying from his hand.

Nightwing stared down at Amber in triumph. The mouse was groaning in pain, twisting. "The fool," he hissed. "What she doesn't know about magic will get her killed."

He whirled and looked at Ben. Ben saw the fat tick, Darwin, clinging to the bat's neck.

"What's wrong with her?" Ben asked. "Did she run out of magic?"

"No," the bat said. "She tried to cast a spell that was a lie. And that can never be done." He looked Ben in the eye and said, "For you see, a magic spell must be born from your innermost desires. It is a wish, given power and force. And when you try to cast a spell that is a lie, one that conflicts with your innermost desires—" the bat aimed a wing at the dazed and wounded mouse, "that is what happens. The magic force turns against you."

Ben worried for Amber, but then he began to understand. "Are you telling me that Amber *can't* turn me back into a human?"

The ugly bat nodded, shook a bit of water and hail off of his wings. "Never. She has grown to like you too much. And so she will want to keep you."

Ben suddenly felt sick with shock. Amber cried out, as if in pain, and Ben saw something odd. There was a light around her, like a pale red fog, that seemed to be leaking from her body. Indeed, as he looked down, he could see tiny bits of fiery light seeming to seep from every pore.

"What? What's happening?" Ben asked.

"It's her shayde," Nightwing said. "The magic will leach it out of her and tear her apart, just as her conflicting desires are tearing her apart."

"Isn't there anything we can do to save her?"

"Save her?" Nightwing said. "Why would you want to? If you save her, she will hold you captive."

"But, I don't want her to die," Ben said.

Amber shrieked in torment, and Ben could see the mist bleeding from her, rising up, turning into a strangely ghostlike mouse shape that looked up toward the sky as if seeking refuge in a distant meadow.

"Her spirit longs for release," Nightwing said. "Let her go."

"*You* can do something," Ben suggested. "You said that you know some magic."

"Perhaps," Nightwing said. "I could save her—for a price." He hesitated, as if thinking what he might want. "How about this? You will serve me. You will become my familiar for a month, and at the end of that time, if your service has pleased me well, I will turn you back into a human."

"Hey," Darwin said, pulling his proboscis from the bat's shoulder. "I thought I was your familiar."

Ben thought about the offer. What did Nightwing mean, *If your service has pleased me well?* What were the responsibilities of a familiar? Didn't he just have to sit there and let the bat drain the magic from him? What could Ben possibly do that would displease the bat? Ben was afraid to make such a deal, but he didn't really see any other choice. And he had to do it now, before Amber died.

"Quickly, now," Nightwing urged Ben. "She's nearly dead already."

"Okay," Ben said. "I'll do it."

"Wait a minute," Darwin told the bat. "You can't be serious about taking this kid on. He doesn't know the first thing about being a familiar. Besides, you can only have one familiar at a time. Where does that leave me?"

Nightwing looked down at the tick and gave him an evil smile that showed his rapacious teeth.

Then the bat leaped toward Amber and inhaled a deep breath. The red glowing fog was sucked into his nostrils. And as it entered the bat's chest, Amber cried out one last time and then went still. She lay in a stupor, unmoving, perhaps even dead, her lips parted as if in pain.

The bat leaned forward, blew toward Amber, and the red haze left his lungs, forming a mist in the air, much like the mist that comes from a warm body on a cold morning.

But this mist moved like something alive, inserting itself between Amber's lips. It bubbled and boiled, shrinking back into her. And when it was gone, she took a deep breath, and lay there, sleeping.

"She'll awaken in time," Nightwing said. The bat turned its glittering black eyes toward Ben. "Now, what shall I do with you? I need a familiar that I can carry." He seemed to think a moment and then smiled cruelly. "Ah, I know."

Without notice, Ben felt a sharp twinge in his side, and suddenly two pairs of extra legs came ripping through his chest. They were monstrous, crablike things as pale as flesh. He had half a dozen segments in each leg, and as he flexed his newfound muscles, the things curled inward. He stared in shock as both his arms and legs began to lose their form, becoming like the other four legs, and then Ben was shrinking, shrinking.

In half an instant, he stared up at the bat, which now did indeed look as large as a dragon.

Ben had turned into a tick.

"Come," Nightwing said, raising one wing up. "Come to me, and I will protect you."

"What have you done to me?" Ben cried.

"Come, taste my blood," Nightwing said. "You will feed from me, even as I feed off of your power."

"But, I don't want to be a tick," Ben cried. "I don't want to drink your blood."

"Nonsense," Nightwing said. "In time, you'll learn to crave it, just as Darwin does now. He wasn't always a tick, you know. He started out life as a dung beetle."

"Dung," Darwin wailed, as if the very word caused an uncontrollable craving. "Ah . . . what I would do for just one little ball of dung."

Ben stood, his many feet rooted to the table, and looked about. Amber was a giant compared with him now, something the size of an elephant. Pizza crumbs that the mice had dropped looked as big as boulders. Indeed, a single ball of hail that had bounced to the table was large enough that it could have crushed him.

Slowly, Ben made his way to the bat. He couldn't figure out how to crawl with so many feet.

Eight legs, he realized, *and all of them are shaking so badly that I can hardly stand*.

So Ben crawled. He got down on his hands and feet and just let his extra legs dangle uselessly as he crawled to his new master.

I won't eat, he promised himself. *I won't eat for a month*. Luckily, his stomach was still full of pizza.

"Cheer up," Nightwing said. "There are worse types of vermin than a tick that you could be." Then he giggled, "Although I really can't think of one."

Ben was still inching across the table when Nightwing leaped forward, grasped him tenderly in a claw, and swept up into the air.

It was a wild ride through the hail, but strangely, none of it seemed to hit the bat, who dodged this way and that as he flew, swerving and dipping, climbing and stalling in the air only to veer off in another direction—all the while letting giant hailstones go whistling by like cannonballs.

Ben glanced down and saw Amber sleeping quietly on the table while the pet shop mice crept out of hiding, making their way toward her. The lights of Dallas, Oregon, were growing small in Ben's sight, shrinking, shrinking.

"Good-bye, Amber," Ben whispered. "You really are the prettiest mouse I've ever seen."

Darwin began to plead, "Okay, boss, I see what's going on. You're done with me. You've got a new buddy. So let me down."

Nightwing shook all over as he laughed evilly, squeaking like a rusty hinge while twisting between the falling balls of hail.

"You're not really going to let me go, are you?" Darwin begged. "Oh, I know what you're thinking."

Suddenly, the bloated tick leaped off of Nightwing, crying out as he fell.

Nightwing swooped, diving toward the tick, and grabbed the poor beast in his mouth. There was a crunching sound as the bat ate his former familiar.

Nightwing gulped the horrible meal down and smiled. Ben clung to the bat's warm, stinky fur, afraid that if he fell, he'd be next on the menu. He was even more afraid of that than he was of the pellets of hail that were whistling past.

He could smell blood flowing through the bat's veins, just beneath the skin. It seemed to call to him.

With a rising sense of helplessness and horror, Ben was swept off into the night.

The next thing that Lady Blackpool knew, the turtle was spinning wildly out of control.

CHAPTER 13

THE SWAMP WITCH

Arriving in the nick of time is good enough and makes life far more entertaining than arriving early.
—LADY BLACKPOOL

LADY BLACKPOOL RODE her flying turtle through the storm. They had been traveling all day at an altitude of nearly three hundred feet, and so the turtle had to climb each time that it reached a hill or cliff, then dip into each valley, thus making for a bumpy ride. Half a dozen times, Sea Foam had retracted his head as he braced for impact with low-flying ducks and geese, and each time that he did so, Lady Blackpool nearly got squished to death.

But she endured it. Rufus Flycatcher was depending on her to save Amber from the enemy—and Lady Blackpool was up to the task.

Still, she was tired. They crossed the snow-covered Cascade Mountain range, diving under the clouds where the night was as dark as a witch's brew. Suddenly, the hail began to fall.

Ahead, Lady Blackpool sensed powerful magics. There were flashes and purple mushroom clouds rising up, clouds that only a powerful mage could see. Lady Blackpool imagined that a battle was going on.

Balls of hail were battering poor Sea Foam's head and flippers, bouncing off him like marbles, and he retracted them as best he could.

"Maybe we should call a halt," Sea Foam said after getting bashed on the noggin by a particularly large hailstone. "I feel like someone has been using my head as a conga drum."

"No," Lady Blackpool urged. "Keep going. We've only got a few more minutes." And it was true. Traveling at two hundred miles per hour, they were nearly to their destination. She pointed down to some lights. "In fact, we only need to get there—to that human village."

"Okay," Sea Foam said with a groan.

It was just then that a horrible blinding light sizzled across the sky. Lady Blackpool felt each of her hairs stand on end, just before the lightning bolt struck.

Sea Foam lighted up, and then his eyes rolled back in his head. The next thing that Lady Blackpool knew, the turtle was spinning wildly out of control.

"Sea Foam," she shouted, trying to wake him, but he was as limp as a dead minnow, and the ground was coming up fast.

Lady Blackpool thrust her paw forward, trying to create something of a force field in order to protect them during the crash, just as they dove over the Willamette River and went careening into a pile of blackberry bushes.

The force field softened the blow as the three-hundred-pound sea turtle ripped through the bushes, plowed into the wet, muddy ground, and skidded into some farmer's wire fence.

Lady Blackpool stood for a moment under the lip of the turtle's shell and breathed a sigh of relief.

Poor Sea Foam was trying to raise his head, but each time that he did, his eyes rolled back, and he'd drop it again.

"Are you going to be okay?" Lady Blackpool asked.

"I couldn't feel more cooked if I was turtle soup," Sea Foam said.

The hail pounded Sea Foam's back. Lady Blackpool didn't dare go out. There was nothing to do but sit in the shelter and wait out the storm.

No sooner had she reached that conclusion than Sea Foam fainted. Up ahead, the magic fireballs had stopped.

"I only hope that I'm not too late," Lady Blackpool whispered.

"The master returns! The master returns!"

CHAPTER 19

THE MUSH ROOM

We should always encourage those around us
to reach their highest potential.
—NIGHTWING

BEN TWISTED AND FLOATED through a dark and loathsome dream. He kept his eyes closed as Nightwing flew, for the trip was jarring and made Ben's stomach turn.

He came awake once to find that the bat had climbed above the storm. Down below him, lightning popped and flashed beneath the black and boiling clouds, while overhead, the stars loomed so close that they threatened to burn him.

Ben could hear the bat muttering as he flew, reciting poetry beneath his breath, his voice alternately hissing and then booming.

But see, amid the mimic rout
A crawling shape intrude!
A blood-red thing that writhes from out
The scenic solitude!
It writhes!—it writhes!—with mortal pangs
The mimes become its food
And seraphs sob at vermin fangs
In human gore imbued.

Out—out are the lights—out all!
And, over each quivering form,
The curtain, a funeral pall,
Comes down with the rush of a storm,
While the angels, all pallid and wan,
Uprising, unveiling, affirm
That the play is the tragedy, "Man,"
And its hero the Conqueror Worm.

Nightwing dipped beneath the clouds again, and in the distance, Ben glimpsed the sea surrounding a rugged jut of land. There was a statue atop the jut, a strange one unlike anything Ben had ever seen. It was an Egyptian god, a jackal, holding a huge brazier above its head—a saucer that at some time far in the past had been filled with fire. Suddenly, Ben realized what the strange statue was—a lighthouse, here at the end of the world.

But then Ben must have passed from a dream into a nightmare, for the bat dove steeply past the statue, down among trees that were bent and twisted into shapes that were so grotesque that they no longer looked like trees. Knotholes gaped like screaming mouths, and Ben felt sure that he saw pain-filled eyes hidden behind the leaves. Ben found himself clinging to the bat in terror, more afraid of the woods than of his vile master. Vines and creepers clung to the demented trees, but these were no ordinary vines. Ben saw lengths of them coil around tree limbs like serpents or crawl upon the ground.

Ben smelled death below. Indeed, strange fungi grew in huge colonies, giving a deathly green glow, and by their quavering light, he spotted an abandoned car surrounded by the grotesque woods. Thorn bushes circled the car, raking the air with thorns as long as daggers.

A strange cry rose up from the broken land, a cry that seemed to be neither human nor animal. Ben looked down and saw a raven with the sharp-nosed face of an evil old man.

The monstrous raven cried, "The master returns! The master returns!"

Other shouts rose from the woods. They might have been cheers of greeting or cries of lament.

Nightwing dove under the trees into a dark grotto where all was shadow. Enormous spiders, as luminous as fireflies, had built nests here, and as the spiders suddenly fluoresced, their webs lit up like gauzy ropes of light.

The bat flapped into a dank cave where hot pools bubbled among rocks that looked strangely like animals trying to flee.

Then Nightwing rose up, flying through a haze over a vast chamber. The lightning spiders were everywhere in here, covering the ceiling so that it shone with luminous webs. And on the floor of the cavern were monstrosities—scorpion-like creatures as big as rats, opossums with heads that sprouted bony armor, toads with eyes that glowed as red as coals. Giant evil-looking worms that buzzed their tails like rattlesnakes and watched Nightwing as if hoping that he'd drop a meal among them.

The cavern reeked of decay. And as Nightwing swooped low, the horrid creatures shouted in unison, "Master returns! Master! Master!"

Nightwing flew up to a rock where an enormous serpent lay, a snake that looked as cruel as a cobra. Its skin glowed sullenly, and upon it was painted the most amazing scene—a child whose world seemed to be melting as he cried in horror.

"Welcome, Master," the snake hissed, rising up to look down on the bat.

"Good evening, Fanglorious," Nightwing said. "I see that you molted while I was gone. How do you like the new skin? Edvard Munch's *The Scream*, I think it's called."

"It's much better," the snake said. "I was getting so tired of that grinning face of Alfred E. Neuman."

"Well, it does suit you," Nightwing told the snake.

All the while as they spoke, the monsters in the cave kept chanting, "Master! Master! Master!"

The bat set Ben on the ground and strode around him, as if anxiously inspecting a new toy.

"Hey, that's not Darwin," Fanglorious said.

"No," Nightwing hissed. "It's not. It's something better." The bat addressed Ben. "Now, my little friend, it is time for a test of your powers. Don't fail me. You know what happens to insects that fail me."

The bat surveyed his cavern and shouted to his minions, "Release the hummers."

Suddenly, a pair of spiders parted their webs, and a humming filled the air. Ben glanced up to see a dozen hummingbirds come swooping from a hole. They darted around the room, first veering, then pausing in midair, ethereal creatures, their emerald-green feathers making them shine like gems come to life.

"Die," Nightwing shouted.

Instantly, the hummingbirds seemed to explode, leaving nothing but feathers drifting in the air. From the horrid mob of creatures on the floor came evil cackling, and the monsters rushed to feed on the remains of the fallen hummingbirds.

Ben gaped in horror. He had never imagined that the bat might use his magical powers for anything so terrible.

Nightwing sighed in satisfaction. "Very nice. Now, we shall put the mush room to good use!"

"Bring forth some prisoners."

There was movement among the mass of grotesque bodies below, a seething as creatures moved aside, and from a pair of holes came two creatures. One of them was a mourning dove, as white as snow. The other was a crab. The dove crept forward timidly, eyeing the monsters around it. The crab scuttled sideways toward them, waving its claws in the air as if to ward off any attack.

"Welcome," Nightwing called down to the prisoners. "Welcome to the Dark Arena. Here in my cavern, we have a saying, 'Extinction is the destiny of the weak.' And tonight, for our amusement, someone is going to become extinct!"

Guffaws of laughter rose from the mob of monsters, along with cheers of "Hooray!" The crab looked up at the dove, his eyestalks waving as he studied his foe. The crab was huge and his claws were massive, while his carapace kept him safely armored.

For its part, the dove just ducked his head and peered around with eyes as black as marbles.

"Hey," Ben said. "That's not fair. There's no way that a dove can beat a crab!"

"Fair?" Nightwing asked. "You want fair? Well, all right then, let's *make* it fair."

From the crowd of monsters, a chant began to arise. "Mush them. Mush them. Mush them."

And with a wave of his clawed wing, Nightwing used his vast powers to make the dove and the crab slide toward one another. Both frightened prisoners tried to pull away, but they were shoved together as if by invisible hands, and in a moment, they pressed against one another firmly.

The dove cried out in pain and the crab wriggled its claws desperately, and all of the denizens of the cave kept shouting, "Mush them. Mush them."

Then the most horrible thing happened. The two creatures seemed to melt into one another, forming a strange and loathsome creature.

What stood below was a horror—a bird with red wings all covered with a crablike carapace. Where the joint of the wings should have been, claws curled out like hooks. Its head displayed armor plates with strange horns. Its chest had segments of armor on it too, and the crab-dove scurried around, his six bony feet clacking on the rocks.

"Hooray!" the monsters all cheered as they looked upon this newly formed horror.

The crab-dove looked at itself in shock, and Nightwing cried out, "Oh, don't be so alarmed. Your disfigurement serves a higher purpose. If you fight well, you will live, and I might even reward you by creating more monsters of the same design to fight under your command in my army. Now bring in this week's champion," Nightwing cried with glee, and the seething mass of monsters moved aside as some evil beast came slithering among them. Ben gulped as it came into view—a sharp-toothed eel, gasping in the air. It had hundreds of powerful little rubbery legs and armor plates running the length of its back. Ben realized with disgust that the eel had been mushed with a centipede.

Cheers arose as the two combatants began to circle one another, each searching for an opening.

The crab-dove looked terrified and kept trying to run, but it didn't seem to know whether it should inch sideways or rush forward, so it tripped over its new feet.

The eelipede responded by whipping its tail around, bashing the helpless creature against some rocks.

Ben gazed down in horror at what was happening and realized that it was like some evil game of *Pokémon*.

No, he thought. *It's more like a cockfight or a dogfight*.

But then someone in the crowd shouted to the eelipede, "Use your poison attack!" And Ben realized that yes, it was exactly like *Pokémon*.

The eelipede lunged and grabbed the crab-dove, lifting it high in the air and hurling it down with a sickly crunch.

There was brief moment of utter silence when the only sound to be heard was the crash of waves upon rock, and then the monsters broke into a wild cheer.

Nightwing drew his huge ears back and raised his wings to cover them protectively while the cavern shook with cheers and applause.

"Good times, eh?" Nightwing shouted to Ben. "I've barely scratched the surface of your power. Oh, we're going to have gobs of fun. Gobs of it!"

He jumped onto a pizza and pried some pineapple out of the hardened cheese.

CHAPTER 15

DOONBARRA

Trouble foreseen is trouble averted.
—Bushmaster

"Gobs of fun," someone was saying in Amber's dream. "Gobs of it." But in the dream, there were cries of pain and death, followed by the roars and shouts of a monstrous applause. Amber awoke with a gasp.

The night was cold and foggy. The lights of Fat Jim's Pizza were low. Only a couple of neon signs in the window still shined. Amber got to her feet and shivered. She felt different somehow—weaker, more vulnerable. She remembered about Ben and a strange dream that she had. She'd been trying to change Ben into a human and then . . .

She peered around. The pet shop mice had fallen asleep on a pizza, huddling together for warmth. They lay there, fast asleep, as if they were pizza toppings ordered by a cat.

Amber thought that she spotted Ben lying asleep with his helmet on, holding his spear like a fallen warrior, with his little grappling hook and ropes thrown over his shoulder.

Only it isn't Ben, Amber realized. *It's Bushmaster.* She recognized the vole by his grizzled fur and short tail.

Amber suddenly realized that no one was keeping watch. She cast her eyes about and saw something under a bush—a blackness, as if a deeper shadow. A creature stood on its rear feet, watching her.

A *ferret!* she thought, gulping in fear. *It must have followed me from the pet shop.*

Suddenly, the creature bounded toward her.

Amber wished that she had Ben's spear and held her paw out, waiting for it to leap into her fingers. But all that happened was that she felt a slight dizziness and a rush of fatigue.

Suddenly the creature bounded into the air and literally flew toward her, landing scant inches away.

"G'day," the creature said, bending down over her. "You've turned into quite the wizard."

Amber finally recognized the creature—a sugar glider. The strange little fellow had come into the pet shop just this past week. He was a shy animal that only came out at night. He could fly like a squirrel but was more closely related to an opossum.

He said in his strange accent, "Spare a bit of tucker for a weary old critter on his walkabout?"

"Food, you mean?" Amber asked. "You want some pizza?"

The sugar glider hopped away and began eating before she could offer him any. He jumped onto a pizza and pried some pineapple out of the hardened cheese. "Hey, this looks like good stuff! Too bad they don't have a few wood beetles on it too."

"I know you," Amber said, "from the pet shop!"

"Nah," the sugar glider said. "I'm not from no pet shop. I'm from Down Under. Name's Doonbarra."

"Under where?" Amber asked.

"Tasmania," Doonbarra said. He stood, with a rapt gleam in his eye. "Now there's a place for you. Rolling hills covered with blue gum trees, the wallabies leaping for joy in fields of kangaroo grass, the wild cockatoos rising up in clouds to cover the sky. Now that's real country. Don't know how you folks can bear living around here."

"Your home sounds nice," Amber agreed. Amber wasn't sure, but she imagined that Doonbarra was big enough and strong enough to give even a cat a good fight. Doonbarra had a deep, gravelly voice, a big voice for such a small creature. Well, small compared with a Doberman. Compared with a mouse, Doonbarra was a giant. And he had strong claws with big sharp nails to match his voice.

"Tell you what," Doonbarra said, leaping forward so that he could stare in her eye. "You cast a spell to take me home, and I'll show you around."

Amber looked at the sugar glider's desperate face and realized that that's why he had been following her. He was desperate to get home. "I'd be happy to take you," Amber admitted. "But I don't even know where Tasmania is. And even if I did, I'm not sure if I could use magic to get there."

"Ah, pooh!" Doonbarra said. "Wizards can do anything. Why, I knew this platypus back home, a lovely girl, really. She used to lay these magic eggs that were just incredible! You could make a wish, crack one open, and out would pop the most amazing things—bits of fresh honeycomb or the scent of a rose or a cow's moo."

Amber got up and looked around as Doonbarra rambled on about magical platypuses and wizardly wombats.

Amber nuzzled Bushmaster awake. "Where's Ben?" she asked.

"Gone," Bushmaster said. As he explained how Ben had been taken, Doonbarra hopped over and listened with keen interest.

Amber didn't remember anything after she'd tried to turn Ben into a human. Now her head spun as Bushmaster explained what a bat was—a mouse that flew at night, hunting insects—and told how the one had stolen Ben away by turning him into a noxious little bloodsucking tick.

"Ben got turned into a tick?" she exclaimed. It seemed too bizarre to be true.

And it's all my fault, she thought. *If only I had turned Ben back into a human, he wouldn't have needed to make a bargain with some evil bat.*

"Ben is in trouble," Bushmaster said. "My gut tells me that he shouldn't have trusted that bat. I've heard rumors. Nightwing is his name, an evil sorcerer. He has a fortress near the ocean at a place called Shrew Hill, and it's filled with evil minions."

"Oh, them evil sorcerers can be trouble," Doonbarra agreed with a wise nod. "We had this bandicoot down at Mole Creek. Believe you me, he caused no small stir. A tree branch fell and nearly killed him, so he went to war with the trees. Gathered up an army of termites to help him. Oh, he had minions. Millions of mealymouthed, menacing minions."

Amber shivered in fear. She asked Bushmaster, "Are you sure this bat was Nightwing?"

"As soon as he was done with his old familiar, Nightwing just gobbled him down," Bushmaster said. "There's only one bat in these parts that is that evil."

"Eating your accomplices—" Doonbarra agreed in shock, "why that's . . . that's poor form!"

"Did you see which way Nightwing went?" Amber asked.

Bushmaster shook his head. "I couldn't see clearly in the dark and the hail, with that bat flapping around back and forth so madly, but I think that he finally went west."

Amber nodded. "I feel horrible having let Ben down. But now he's gone, and I have no idea how to find him."

"Oh, that's easy," Doonbarra said. "You want to find him, all you've got to do is find the nearest newt. Look into his eyes, and they'll show you where Ben is."

"What?" Amber asked.

"Don't even need a spell. Just do them a favor, and they'll use their own magic to show you what you want," Doonbarra said. "Learned it from an aborigine up by Cradle Mountain."

Amber's mouth fell open in surprise. Here was someone who knew about magic. "But even if I did find Ben, what can I do for him?"

"Can't help you with that," Doonbarra said. "I don't know the first thing about how to pry a tick off of an evil sorcerer. Though I do seem to remember something about rubbing alcohol. Or was it matches?"

Amber was filled with despair. Nightwing had been right. She hadn't wanted to turn Ben back into a human. Her mind might have said yes, but her heart told her no.

Amber desperately wanted to go find Ben.

But even if I found him, what could I do against a powerful sorcerer?

She looked at the huddled forms of the mice, nuzzled together like round boulders in a small stream. She had a responsibility to Ben, and with all of her heart she wanted to set things right, but she had a responsibility to her friends too. Old Barley Beard had told her that it was her destiny to free the mice of the world. It was to be her life's work.

Now she'd set a few mice free, but free to do what? They had no home, no shelter. They knew nothing about how to forage in the meadows or dig a burrow or hide from hawks and pine snakes. Had she freed them only to let them die in the wilderness?

No, she decided. *I'll have to find a home for them*.

"Bushmaster," Amber said. "Do you think that Old Vervane will take my friends in? Teach them how to feed themselves and keep from being eaten?"

"Of course," Bushmaster said. "He loves being a know-it-all."

"Okay, then," she said. "If the bat went west and we're going west, then we'll drop the pet shop mice off with Vervane and go after Ben."

Amber trudged over to the nearest pizza and began to shout, "Wake up! It's time to go. The owls have gone to roost, and the hawks have yet to wake. It's time for us mice to travel."

Amber stopped after she spoke. She realized how much she had just sounded like Vervane.

I've grown in the past two days, she thought.

The pet shop mice woke as she poked their fat tummies with her nose, and then they filed off into the shadows.

* * *

The pet shop mice spent the morning in damp travel, slogging through fields where rainwater pooled among the grass. Mud puddles seemed like lakes to the mice, and water was everywhere, which made the travel safer in some ways. For with the intermittent rain, the cats and hawks both stayed undercover, leaving the mice to travel in safety.

The only danger they faced was when they crossed some railroad tracks. They didn't go over them, but instead elected to go under, traveling through a drainage pipe. Even then, a train came rumbling overhead, making the ground shake as if the world would tear apart.

Then the most horrible thing happened. The train blew its whistle. The shrill noise was horrifying, and several of the mice, who were already weakened from travel, fainted at the sound.

Amber and Bushmaster had a hard time reviving them.

"You have to watch out in the mornings," Bushmaster said as he and Amber ushered the injured mice from the pipe. "Loud noises after dawn can be dangerous for a mouse. Your body knows that you should be asleep, and so a noise that wouldn't bother you during the night can leave you stunned or even dead if it comes near dawn."

Amber hadn't known that, and now she filed it away in her memory. It made sense when she thought about it. There were times, early in the morning, when sounds seemed unnaturally loud to her ears, loud enough to leave her irritated and angry.

By noon, the sun had come out and the mice had reached higher ground. But still the going was slow, for the world was filled with wonders that the pet shop mice had to investigate—dewdrops and ladybugs, wild roses and old green bottles.

Bushmaster and Amber led the mice carefully. Hop, stop, and look.

Without her magic, Amber was just another mouse. And her responsibility weighed heavily on her.

* * *

It was completely by accident that Doonbarra spotted a newt that afternoon.

"Over here," Doonbarra called, as they were climbing the hills above the millpond. They found him—a lizard with a chocolate brown back and an orange belly—in a small clearing covered with moss, in a place where rills of rainwater tumbled over small stones beneath a canopy of wild blue mountain orchids. The newt was struggling to tug a worm from the ground. He had it in his mouth, and both the newt and the worm were grunting from the battle.

Amber desperately wanted to please the newt, so she said, "Here, let me help with that."

She grabbed the worm and pulled it from the ground like a slimy rope. The worm cried as the newt gulped it down, "Help, I'm a sentient being! I think, therefore I am. And I am being swallowed."

"Ah, that was a fine worm," the newt said as the worm went wriggling to its doom. "Sturdy and juicy, with just a hint of compost. I thank you."

"You're welcome," Amber replied. Then she waited, wondering how to bring up her question. "Uh, I'm looking for an evil bat, a sorcerer who took my friend."

The newt got a faraway look in his golden eyes, and his slit pupils constricted. He nodded and whispered in a deep voice, "Three answers you may have of me: ask what is now, what shall come, or what may be."

Three answers? Amber wondered. *Ask what* is?

"Okay," Amber replied. "I want to free the mice of the world, and my friend Ben is one of them. But how are they bound, and where can I find them?"

Amber worried. Technically, she had just asked two questions, and she was afraid that the newt would notice. She looked deep into the newt's eyes and watched as they suddenly turned red and glassy.

Then it seemed to Amber that she was flying high above the world, a colorful ball of blues and greens with white clouds above. And she saw the mice of the world in their cages. Thousands of mice. Hundreds of thousands of mice. Millions and billions of mice.

She saw them as if in a vision—a sea of mice, white and brown and black, each of them yearning for freedom.

They were everywhere. In cities and towns that spread from the ice sheets of the north to the far Antarctic.

But as Amber peered, she looked down into the deserts over America and saw hordes of mice on the march. They were coming from everywhere, wild mice, cunning in the ways of stealth and evasion.

They were marching toward a dark hole, like a great cavern in the earth. But even the newt's magic vision could not show Amber where they were going.

It was as if the darkness, the hole itself, were aware of Amber.

And as she watched, she realized that many of the mice that she saw hopping through tufts of desert grass or scampering over rocks were barely alive.

Many of them looked haggard, their frames weak from lack of food, as if they were starving. But the worst were more than starved.

Amber could see flesh rotting away from their skulls and bones showing through patches of fallen hair.

Is this a symbol? she wondered. *Am I to free the mice from death? Or is there really a dark hole that they are going to?*

Amber shivered inside, recalling Vervane's warnings. The mice around here were gone and had been leaving all winter.

No, this wasn't a metaphor for death. This was a real place, and the mice were being drawn to it.

Amber peered toward the blackness, the great hole. It was in a desert of red rock, in a place ringed with sharp stones, like worn teeth.

She tried to move toward it and thought she saw shapes in the darkness. Foxes and owls, perhaps.

There are more than just humans to deal with, Amber realized. *There's something else here—sorcery.*

And then the vision faded, and she saw Ben, an ugly little tick huddling among the reddish fur of a vile-looking creature with wings and huge ears. *A bat*, Amber realized. Ben looked miserable, clinging to its fur.

The bat was mushing creatures together, mixing quails with slugs and leeches with spiders, creating an army that would shake the balance of the world. Indeed, he had just finished mushing a new monstrosity.

A huge rattlesnake was half slithering, half walking across the floor. It was a dozen feet long and had the wings of an eagle and an eagle's talons and sharp beak, but the body of a snake.

"Behold, my masterpiece," Nightwing cried, "the Conqueror Worm!"

Suddenly from the cave came the cries of Nightwing's monstrous minions, yammering for blood, howling for war. The bat laughed maniacally even as he wrapped his wings over his ears to protect them from the harsh noise.

Amber felt a tug in her mind, and the newt's voice came to her now, "Three answers you have had from me," the newt whispered. "None are left unto thee."

"Urp," Amber said. So the newt had noticed. Not only had he noticed that she had asked two questions, but he had provided three answers—showing her not just Ben, but also the mice in cages around the world and the mice that were being drawn into the shadow.

Amber felt as if she were being pulled away from Ben, back from his hole, back through the Weird Wood of slithering vines and poisonous nettles and piles of bones that surrounded Nightwing's fortress beneath Shrew Hill.

She kept pulling back and back through endless forests and over rugged mountains, past churning rivers and limitless lakes, until she found herself standing beside the newt.

Amber's heart seemed to stop as the vision faded. A cry of despair rose from her throat as she realized, *I could never walk that far. I'll never make it.*

"Three answers you may have of me: ask what is now, what shall come, or what may be."

CHAPTER 16

THE EYE OF NEWT

He who is best prepared wins his fight
before he ever sets foot on the battlefield.
—NIGHTWING

INSIDE NIGHTWING'S CAVE, the monsters were finally going to sleep.

Nightwing had stayed up all day, herding in prisoners to create new monstrosities and then pitting them against one another until he'd created his ultimate warrior—the Conqueror Worm.

Only then did he tell his minions, "Go search the forests. Bring me eagles and rattlesnakes, a thousand of each! And with them I will build an army that all of the forces of SWARM cannot repel."

Ben felt sickened by the barbarity of the display, the endless bloodshed.

He wanted to run away, but he'd seen what happened to Darwin when he tried to escape. So instead, Ben took a little comfort in knowing that one day was almost done. If he had to serve Nightwing for a month, that meant that he only had twenty-nine days left to go.

Many of the monsters went out that night to hunt for snakes and eagles. Ben suspected that in the morning, Nightwing would begin creating a whole new race of monsters to fight his war. And within a day or two, they'd go to war.

Right now, the cave was relatively empty. Only a few guards remained.

Before they went to sleep, Nightwing ordered Fanglorious the snake, "Bring me a fresh newt!"

In moments, a rubbery brown lizard was squirming in the snake's jaws, trying to escape. The snake wriggled up to Nightwing and dropped the lizard at his feet. The newt cowered before Nightwing and said, "Eat me and you'll die! My skin is poisonous, you know!"

"I know," Nightwing said. "But it's not your skin that I want, just your eye. Now, will you show me what I want, or will you make me rip it from its socket?"

The newt stared blankly, then said in a deep voice, "Three answers you may have of me: ask what is now, what shall come, or what may be."

"Show me my ancient enemy," Nightwing commanded, "Rufus Flycatcher, the High Wizard of SWARM"

The newt's eyes glowed fiery green. Ben peered into them.

He saw a gorgeous scene. It was sunset in a swamp far, far away. Green dragonflies cruised lazily through skies painted gold from a setting sun, while cypress trees cast blue shadows upon the dark water.

Frogs were singing everywhere—croaking so loudly that to Ben it sounded as if he were in a football stadium. There were leopard frogs, bull-frogs, green frogs, tree frogs, spring peepers, car-penter frogs. The calls were so loud and insistent and varied, Ben had never heard anything like it.

The vision zoomed in, down around the roots of a huge cypress tree. There on the cypress knees—knobs of wood that poked up from the black water—sat a handsome bullfrog. Baby alligators patrolled the waters behind him like sentries, while a beautiful white heron watched the bank above, and a pair of turtles—large cooters—sunned on a log nearby. Fireflies danced in the air around his head, their green lights dipping and rising.

Ben had a terrible longing to take a jar and catch the fireflies.

Rufus Flycatcher was busily instructing some young frogs, most of which hadn't even lost their tails yet, about the difficulties in repairing the damaged wings of fireflies.

"The problem," Rufus was saying, "is that fire-flies aren't real flies. If y'all look close, you'll see that they're beetles, and like any beetle, the real wings are hidden beneath an armored shell, called the *elytra*. So these wings, constantly banging agin' this shell, get worn out quicker than a but-terfly bucking against the wind of a tornado . . ."

"Perfect," Nightwing chuckled upon seeing the old bullfrog. "This looks just perfect." Suddenly the bat hissed a loud curse, then magnified his voice as he addressed the frog, "Rufus, I'm coming for you."

Through the newt's eye, Ben could hear the bat's words repeated, only there in the swamp the voice seemed to come from everywhere, booming from the sky, bouncing from the waters, filling every corner of the cypress forest.

The fireflies dipped in the air, startled from their flight, while young frogs and tadpoles croaked in fear and leaped for the safety of the water. Even the alligators dived for safety.

But Rufus Flycatcher boldly held his ground, sitting on a mossy cypress knee while green algae floated all around him. "Nightwing?" Rufus said. "So, you're still alive? I figured for sure that you'd be toasting like a marshmallow in you-know-where by now."

"I'm more alive than you are," Nightwing said. "Your time has come."

"You still runnin' that school of yours, SADIST? Not much of a magic school, from what I hear. What kind of magic do you teach?"

"Like most schools," Nightwing admitted, "we don't profess to teach much at all."

"You know, you're one sick puppy," Rufus said. "It's all that evil in you, poisoning you. I tried to heal you of it once. But you clung to it like a baby possum clinging to its mama's belly. Now, if'n you'd free yourself of evil, you'd be a whole lot better off."

"Why, I thank you for your concern, my old master. But I don't want to be healed. I like being a sick puppy. It's the only thing that I really excel at."

Rufus Flycatcher shook his head sadly. "Once, there was a time when you were a man, a man who could cast a spell over an audience with just the sound of your voice. You'd stand there and recite a poem and folks would just gasp in amazement. Women would throw themselves at you and swoon at your feet. What I want to know is whatever happened to that feller?"

"Ah, well," Nightwing said, "Poets have fallen out of favor in the past hundred years."

The fireflies were still bobbing in the air around Rufus. They brightened a little, believing that the danger was gone.

Nightwing said, "I'll be seeing you soon. You'd better get some rest. You'll need it." Then, in a falsely sweet voice he offered, "Here, let me turn out the lights for you."

And with that, Nightwing hissed a second curse. The fireflies exploded in midair and went raining down into the water, leaving trails of smoke and debris in the air until they hit the brackish pool, sizzling.

"You can't scare me. I'm from Texas!" Rufus said in a challenging tone. "I got warts on my armpit that are scarier than you!" He let out a strange croak, which started deeply, causing the whole cave to thunder and shake from the sound. But as the croak ended, it rose to a piercing shriek that caused Nightwing to hiss and throw his wings up over his ears.

The bat's eyes got wide with terror, as if the continued shrieking would kill him. In desperation, Nightwing waved his wing.

Instantly, the newt's eye cleared, and the vision faded.

Nightwing stood for a moment, trembling in pain, trying to compose himself. Ben realized that the bat's ears had been too sensitive to withstand the bullfrog's sudden assault.

Ben was still gasping in shock at the murder of the fireflies. Though he had gone the whole day without eating, he felt as if he would be sick.

Ben crawled to the edge of the rock and began to gag, remembering the fireflies burning in the water.

Nightwing turned on him and angrily stalked closer. "What, you don't want me to kill the little froggy?"

Ben shook his head sadly.

"You don't like what I'm doing with your power?" Nightwing demanded.

Ben looked up, frightened, and shook his head.

Nightwing snarled, "What kind of tick are you? A luna-tick? A roman-tick? Or are you just fran-tick?"

Ben didn't answer. He sat there, squirming, until Nightwing shouted, "Your attitude displeases me. One day shall be added to your term of service!"

Ben's heart froze. He had dared to hope that in twenty-nine days he would be free. But Nightwing had just made it an even thirty again.

The bat sneered at him, and Ben could sense the creature's game. For every day that Ben served, the bat would think up some excuse to keep him a day longer. Ben would never be able to serve Nightwing well enough to get free.

I'm his slave, Ben realized. *I'm his slave forever.*

The very thought made all eight of Ben's legs so weak that he collapsed to the ground like a rock, his legs clattering around him like broken sticks.

The owl grabbed her in its talons, and Amber feared that it would crush her.

THE FLIGHT OF THE OWL

Wake up to the miracles that happen all around you.
We grow old only when we lose our sense of wonder.
—RUFUS FLYCATCHER

BY NOON, AMBER COULD TELL that the journey to Ben's house was definitely going to take more than a day. The pet shop mice hiked through the fields all day, skirting puddles and temporary creeks, and moved only as quickly as the slowest mouse.

And the mice were slow indeed. They had to stop to ponder every wonder—the cloud-colored throat of a morning glory flower, the sight of ducks flying in a V. They took baths in the warm rain and let themselves dry in the sun. They nibbled on nettles and feasted on peppermint and wild strawberries.

In her spare time, Amber asked Bushmaster and Doonbarra all about bats and learned far too little. It seemed that they were much like mice, but that they flitted about at night, hunting mosquitoes and other gnats. But the most interesting thing that Amber learned was that they could not see well. In the daylight, the sun was too bright, and at night there was often no light. So they guided themselves by sound, emitting high shrieks and chitters, then listening to the tiny echoes.

With such powerful ears, Amber thought, *a bat should practically be able to hear you think*.

No wonder Nightwing had covered his ears when his minions had cheered during the battle.

All during the day, Amber studied and thought and kept watch, worrying for the safety of her friends.

That night, all twenty-seven mice, one vole, and one sugar glider found shelter in a hollow oak tree where they could sleep among the dry leaves. The clouds overhead drifted west and the moon came out, a bright silver ball, and there in the cavernous tree beneath the starlight, Doonbarra told scary stories about ravenous Tasmanian devils and the ghost of a raven that went about stealing the souls of mice to decorate its nest with, until all of them were so frightened that their whiskers stood on end. Then he lightened the mood by telling them a story about an echidna named Sucky Nose who—but the story got bogged down when the mice began asking what an echidna was. Doonbarra explained that an echidna was a small animal that looked like a hedgehog but that it laid eggs, had wicked spines all over its body, and had a long nose like a straw that it stuck in the ground to lick up ants. He explained that echidnas had poisonous spurs on their feet, and that once the babies hatched, they would simply latch onto their mother's skin and begin sucking so hard that milk would come out right through the echidna's hide.

By then the mice all realized that Doonbarra had been lying to them all along with his strange tales of Tasmanian devils and spirit ravens, and now they were rolling on the ground, laughing as he invented the strange echidna.

"But I'm tellin' the truth," Doonbarra shouted. "There really *are* echidnas!"

"Yeah," Bushmaster laughed. "And they live on the moon—with your mother!" All of the mice rolled on the ground and laughed at that.

It was in the midst of this that Amber suddenly felt a chill rush over her. Shadows moved in the darkness, just outside the oak tree.

She whirled and cried, "Watch out," to the other mice.

But in the frail moonglow, all that she saw were voles—a tribe of them, each carrying a needle, the silver starlight and moonlight gleaming from their small spears.

"Hah!" one of them cried. "We sure scared you!"

Amber gaped. She recognized that voice. It was Meadowsweet, one of the voles from behind Ben's house.

Amber found herself suddenly breathing easier.

"You sure did scare me," she laughed.

The voles hopped up and peered into the hollow of the tree.

"What are you doing?" Amber asked.

"We came hunting for you," Meadowsweet said.

Bushmaster pounced forward, his helmet terrifying to behold, and studied his brothers and sisters. "*You* came all of this way?"

"Sure," Meadowsweet said. "We weren't afraid."

Another vole chimed in. "We've got spears now! Other animals are afraid of us."

"Yeah," Meadowsweet said. "We attacked Domino this morning and chased him around so much that he finally climbed a telephone pole and yowled his head off. Now, every cat for a mile around knows what to expect if they mess with us."

And so, laughing and joking, the voles entered the hollow of the oak and joined the party.

Soon, Amber could hear them teaching their silly songs to the mice and laughing in the easy way that voles had, and Amber went alone out in the moonlight.

She felt at peace for the first time today. If the voles really were putting the fear of small animals into the local cats, then she felt sure that the pet shop mice would make it home in relative safety.

And even Doonbarra was there to protect them. The mice, tonight, were as safe as they could be.

Amber went out from under the oak and peered up at the moon. It was silver, and the shadows on its face made it look as if something had been burrowing in it. The stars were glimmering gems.

There, with the wind moving across the fields as quiet as a baby's breath, Amber felt more at ease.

Back in the hole, she could hear Meadowsweet talking loudly. "You haven't heard of Windborne? Why, he's only the most famous mouse that ever lived!"

And suddenly the mice fell silent and listened expectantly as the young vole began telling the story of young Windborne, how a weasel had dug into Windborne's home and tried to eat him and his younger brothers and sisters while his mother was out foraging.

But the weasel was too large and got stuck in the narrow hole. Windborne had begun trying to throw up dirt in order to block the tunnel, digging so fast that the weasel, whose snout was only an inch from Windborne's tail, suddenly began having a coughing fit. Wedged as he was between the rocks, the weasel couldn't get a breath and finally suffocated. Thus began the legend of Windborne, who slew a deadly weasel while he was hardly more than a kitten himself, and who went on to become one of the great legends of mousedom.

Amber listened and somehow felt uprooted. She'd lost much by being born in a cage. She didn't even know her own history. Indeed, she'd never heard a single tale about mouse legends, and it made her wonder what kinds of stories others might tell about her someday.

My *story has just begun*, she realized.

And yet now she had to face Nightwing, and if things went ill, her story would end practically before it had begun.

Amber noticed an old stump nearby, tall, its sides covered in moss, while bits of bark rose up like jagged teeth around its sides. Morning glory climbed around its sides, as pale and translucent as clouds in the moonlight.

Wondering what the view from up there might look like, Amber hopped over to the stump, then climbed up the slick moss, finding fingerholds in the grooves of the bark.

When she reached the top, Amber stared down in wonder. The stump was completely hollow inside, the bark covering it like a shell. Inside the hollow stump, a pool of glassy water had formed. And since the moon was shining straight from above, she could see its reflection and her reflection there in the pool. There was a tiny water plant there, a broad leaf floating.

But it was Amber's reflection that caught her attention. She had never seen herself before, except to catch a bit of her own distorted reflection in another mouse's eyes. Now, she looked down and gasped.

I am pretty, she realized. *I'm very pretty*.

She turned this way and that, looking critically at her own tail, her shiny coat, the gleam of starlight in her eyes.

Why didn't Ben ever notice? she wondered.

"It's because you are a mouse," she told herself. Of course, he had said that she was pretty just before she tried to turn him back into a human, but Amber assumed that he said it only to make her feel better.

Everything was quiet, but suddenly in the distance, Amber heard a single cricket raise its voice in song.

Amber wondered where Ben might be.

"Ah, there you are," someone said. It was an old woman's voice, scratchy and full of hisses. Amber started so hard that she nearly fell down into the water.

She whirled and saw a small mouselike creature clinging to the lip of the stump. It was dark in color, almost as black as night, and had a long pointy nose and a very short tail.

"I've come a long way to see you," the creature said. "Rode a turtle over the Rockies and almost had you when a lightning bolt lit on him and we crashed."

"You've come to see me?"

"And got here just in the nick of time, it seems," the creature said. "My name is Blackpool. Lady Blackpool, and I was sent here by the good Rufus Flycatcher, the High Mage of SWARM. There is a place for you there, if you would like to go—a place where you can study the magical arts and master them, as is your destiny."

"I don't understand," Amber said. "I don't know a thing about magic."

"All wise folk were born ignorant," Lady Blackpool said. "Now, listen up. I've seen in a vision that you must take a long trip this night and must fight a great battle at dawn. But there are some things that you need to know."

She came and sat down next to Amber and peered into the dark water, gazing at their reflection.

"The first thing that you need to know is this: magic is everywhere."

Amber followed Lady Blackpool's gaze out across the fields. Rye grass and oats shot up everywhere, along with tangled vines and wildflowers. Here and there, wild Indian tobacco and ferns towered above the grasses. From this height, Amber could even see a forest rising over the hills and the millpond surrounded by cattail rushes.

"See that?" Lady Blackpool said. "There's life everywhere, everywhere that you look. Some places have more life—huge trees rising up in forests, deep roots under the soil. Some places have less life—desert sands where nothing can grow. Magic is that way too. It's everywhere. A bit here, a bit there. Some places have almost no magic at all, and in some places, the magic is as thick as a forest. We can't see it, can't taste it. But sometimes . . . sometimes you can *feel* it."

Amber pondered this for a long moment. "But, if the magic is everywhere, then that means that I should always have *some* magic power, right?"

"Almost always," Lady Blackpool said. "All that you have to do is find a place where magic is strong and let it cling to you."

"But how will I know when I've found one?"

Lady Blackpool peered far away. "There are places in this world," she said, "where the magic is thick in the air. Sometimes, when you're in one of those places, your mind might be racing so fast that you don't even notice. But if you slow down and listen . . ."

Amber thought for a long moment. Had she ever been to such a place?

She wasn't sure.

"So," Amber said, "all that I really need to do to gain some power is to find a magic place? And so . . . if I travel far enough, I should stumble on one, right?"

"That's the long and short of it," Lady Blackpool said. "Most of us wizards are always traveling, always looking for a little patch of magic to keep us going. We're a lean bunch, haggard, but smart. Kind of pathetic. But some of us settle down. You're a lucky one, to have a nice powerful familiar like Ben. Someday you'll be able to just settle down and let the magic flow to you."

Amber shivered to think of what a treasure she had lost in Ben, and she looked at this strange little dark ball of fur and wondered what kind of creature it was. Not a mouse, not a vole. It almost looked like a mouse that had been badly mangled, and Amber didn't dare say anything, lest the old wizardess get embarrassed.

"Once you find a little magic spot," Lady Blackpool said, "you have to conserve your power. Using magic takes energy. Using big magic takes a lot of energy. When you turned Ben into a mouse, you used more energy than most mages would in a lifetime."

"Really?" Amber asked.

"That's right. So, for example, if you wanted to eat a blueberry, you could make one pop out of thin air. But that would take a lot of energy. Instead, you might simply wish that you knew where to find a blueberry—or maybe you might wish to find any food at all. For you see, knowledge comes easy. It doesn't take much energy to change your mind."

Lady Blackpool fell silent.

As Amber stood peering into the water, she suddenly realized that she had been lost in a daydream for some time. The air around her seemed unnaturally still and silent, and with a profound sense of wonder, Amber realized that this was a magic place.

Perhaps I should go swimming in the pool, Amber thought. *That way the magic will rub off on me*.

But even as she thought it, a huge shadow fell over her, and the light in the pool winked out.

"Owl," Amber cried. She looked up, just in time to see a huge owl swooping down on her, its eyes flashing golden in the moonlight. Its enormous wings spread out, casting a shadow that covered the world. It was ready to take her in its talons.

Amber raised her needle, ready to defend herself, and just as quickly, she realized what she had to do.

"Carry me to Nightwing's cave," she commanded, letting the force of her wish bind the owl into her service.

The owl grabbed her in its talons, and for half a moment, Amber feared that it would crush her. But instead it only gripped her lightly and then pounded its wings as it thundered up into the stars.

From down below, Lady Blackpool shouted, "Good-bye, Amber. Fight wisely! I'd come with you, but I'm too tired to go off and fight an army tonight."

Amber glanced down to see the strange little creature sitting there on the log at the side of the pool.

In seconds, Amber was airborne, and she realized that she wasn't going to die.

She looked down and saw the great oak tree spreading above the fields. From up high, everything looked brighter than it had below. The stars lit the skies above, and the moon lit the silver fields below. Amber watched the oak tree. The mice inside were safe, Amber felt certain. They had the voles with their spears, and now they had Lady Blackpool to guard them too.

So she merely rested, clutching her spear, thinking about what lay ahead as the owl soared high, taking her above the silver clouds where the sky was full of wind and falling stars.

Ben faded out of consciousness, growing ever weaker. The hunger was numbing.

CHAPTER 18

A TICK WELL FED

Food may give life, but it is hope and love that give meaning to our lives.
—Rufus Flycatcher

As THE MOON SAILED through the sky, Nightwing's minions searched abroad, bringing creatures in from the forest so that Nightwing could expand his army.

Several times during the night, Ben was awakened as eagles were brought, beaks bound tightly with ropes braided from sharp-thorned blackberry vines. Snakes were dragged in, hissing and rattling.

And each time a pair was found, Nightwing would immediately mush the two together, forming a new monster to the gleeful howls and yammers of his minions.

Ben climbed on Nightwing's belly and just squatted, his eight legs hooked into the bat's fur, and dropped in and out of consciousness during the night.

He was too tired to stay awake and too tormented to sleep.

In his dreams, Ben sat as a mute witness to the sight of death, the sounds of battle, the cries of torment. When he woke, it was even worse, for the odor of blood and gore saturated the cave. And though the scent nauseated Ben, the smell of blood also aroused him.

A tick knows the smell of food. Ben fought the craving. But the worst part was that he felt sure that if he remained a tick for long, his hunger would get the better of him, and he would feast upon Nightwing's blood.

Sort of like a vampire in reverse, he thought.

Ben faded out of consciousness, growing ever weaker. The hunger was numbing, driving all reason from his mind.

I can't go on living like this, Ben realized. *It would be better to die than to live with this hunger.*

And with that realization, a plan began to take form in his mind.

Without me, Nightwing would be weakened, Ben realized. *He wouldn't be able to carry out his stupid war. He wouldn't be able to mush helpless animals, turning them into monsters.*

All that I have to do is run away.

But what then? Ben wondered.

I could sneak out of here at dawn, after everyone has gone to bed, and go back to Amber. Maybe, if I'm lucky, she'll turn me back into a mouse.

Ben realized that it would be a long trip. He was at the coast, some sixty miles or more from his home. Walking home as a human would have been a huge job, but trying to do it as a tick, a tick who hadn't even figured out how to use all eight legs?

It was hopeless.

I'll never make it, Ben realized. *I'll die long before I reach home*.

And then with finality, he realized, *And I don't really care. I'd rather be dead than a tick well fed.*

* * *

The owl needed to rest that night. Climbing high in the thin air to skirt over the mountaintops was a tough job, even for a gnarly, old owl.

And so it was near dawn when the great horned owl glided down over the dark pine forests toward the gray ocean. It skirted just above the treetops as it headed toward the strange lighthouse atop Shrew Hill. Ahead, gnarled little leafless trees raised their branches as if in despair, and Amber could see hot water creating a fog that flowed through the woods, hiding them.

"Shrew Hill," the owl said as they approached. "I see guardians about, monsters in the wood. But the defenses are built for a large-scale assault. A single mouse, approaching warily, might get through."

Amber had been thinking all night. She didn't know how much magic power she had left. For all that she knew, she'd used it all just to hijack the owl.

So she didn't want to confront Nightwing. No, she'd have to sneak in, find Ben, and then carry him back out.

If Nightwing slept during the day, then Amber imagined that it would be safest to wait until well after dawn.

So when the owl dropped her at the edge of the strange woods, Amber thanked him and set him free. The sun was just rising, and as the owl took off and beat his mighty feathers, soaring over the haunted wood, Amber heard the cries of beasts as they shouted warning, "Intruder! There's an owl loose!"

She heard the sounds of large creatures lumbering through the brush, as if to give chase to the owl, and silently she thanked the good bird for the diversion. Then she moved forward warily, gripping her spear, keeping under heavy cover—hop, stop, and look.

* * *

Dawn stole slowly through the sky that morning, golden light creeping over the earth, creating a glow that outlined the opening to the cave.

The monsters that lived in Nightwing's shadow had been up all night, celebrating as each new eagle and snake was mushed into one. And so now the cave grew quiet, except for the snores of sleeping creatures.

Ben had been clinging to the fur on Nightwing's belly. Now he peered around, looking for signs of danger.

Most of the monsters lay on their backs or sides, breathing deeply, perhaps emitting a small growl as they dreamed or scratched wildly at fleas. But it wasn't possible to tell if all of the monsters were asleep. The lightning spiders had let their lights burn low, but their faceted eyes gleamed in the darkness, and Ben imagined that if he even touched one of their shiny webs, the spiders would come darting out to meet him. And there were snakes and other monsters that had no eyelids, so that if they slept, Ben had no way of knowing.

He looked about, then leaped down from Nightwing. It would have been a mighty leap if he were a human, for Nightwing was clinging to the ceiling, and when Ben jumped, he dropped hundreds of times his own height.

He landed on a rock, his eight legs catching his weight nicely.

Then he began to scurry for the exit.

Monsters guarded the way: possum-lizards with sharp teeth and evil smiles, porcupine-weasels that could run faster than the wind, scorpion-skunks that smelled almost as deadly as their stings.

And all of them were so much larger than Ben. He had to creep among them, his eight tiny feet clattering over the stone.

At first, he was afraid that they might wake and see him. But then he realized that if one of the monsters even just rolled over on top of him, it could be disastrous.

So he sneaked past the creatures until he reached a pool of steaming water.

He jumped in and began to swim as best he could, his eight legs in a tangle. He prayed as he swam, "Don't let there be any fish in these pools. Not even a guppy. Please."

He swam for what seemed a long hour, until, exhausted, he reached the far end of the pool.

By now, the sun had risen, and the golden glow that had encircled the front of the cave was strong and silver. Ben could smell pine trees outside and the salty scent of the ocean.

He scrambled over a long expanse of rock into the sunlight, afraid that at any moment, some lizard guard would rush up and gobble him down.

He was at the mouth of the cave, looking down over the wild woods, the twisted trees and cruel vines. Then he heard a deep voice, a growl, at his back. "What are you doing out here? Trying to run away?"

Ben turned, and his heart sank. There, just behind him at the mouth of the cave, slithered a creature half eagle, half rattlesnake. Ben peered up at the cruel beak and golden eyes of the Conqueror Worm.

The snake-eagle rose high in the air, searching, searching . . .

CHAPTER 19

A SONG FOR A FRIEND

Being a good friend to another can be a challenging and ennobling undertaking.
—BUSHMASTER

AMBER WAS RACING through the brush, hop, stop, and look. She didn't know much about plants, but these ones looked sickly. The trees and bushes had mouths that gaped, and in some of them, she even thought that she saw teeth. Indeed, every one of them looked like some kind of animal—a dog, a mink—that had been caught racing from the cave and was then transformed into a plant, so that an animal's body formed the trunk of a tree or prickly bush, while branches and limbs sprouted from its head and back.

Knotholes were mouths and eyes. Twisted roots became feet, binding the creatures to the ground.

Amber hopped forward, peering around a bush. She spotted a rabbit nibbling on some brush, but saw that it was a strange rabbit with short ears and fangs.

It lifted its head and tasted the air for a scent, then went hopping over her head in a great rush. She was just about to move again when she spotted a vine wriggling. It looked like a bit of blackberry vine, complete with leaves, but slithered along a limb, its cruel thorns rasping. It lifted a tiny head, a single green leaf, and Amber spotted little nubs upon it—unblinking eyes. Then the vine monster wriggled up a tree, as if seeking a place to sun itself.

Everything is alive here, she warned herself. *Even the bushes have eyes. Even things that should be dead are alive*.

Her heart hammering in her throat, Amber hopped a few paces. She hid in the shadow of a wild cucumber vine, its pale purple flowers open to the daylight, and watched the path ahead.

A creature—the fanged rabbit—went barreling through the brush.

Amber waited, heart pounding, until it left the trail, and then she went scampering forward, only to find that her foot was tangled.

She turned and gasped. The wild cucumber had snagged her rear ankle with a tender green shoot, and as she tried to pull free, its leaves hissed at her.

Amber spun and stabbed with her little spear, piercing the vine.

Suddenly the tiny trumpet-shaped flowers all constricted and began to emit shrill whistles.

A warning call!

There was nothing that she could do now but run.

She pulled herself free of the vine and went hopping down the trail. She heard a thump as something huge came crashing through the brush ahead, and she jumped aside just in time. A hairy creature with black stripes on its back went thundering past, bounding on long legs.

A *chipmunk-toad*, Amber realized.

She was drawing near the cave now, she knew. She could hear the tinkle of water as it flowed over small stones.

She raced up to a poor misshapen bush and stood hiding in the canopy of its leaves, looking for the opening of the cave. And there she saw a sight that nearly stopped her heart.

An insect stood in the golden sunlight, just at the mouth of the cave. Above it, a monstrous snake spread gold-and-white wings and rose up, like a cobra, to peer down upon the insect.

Ben!

Amber heard movement in the brush. The cucumber vine was still blowing its shrill whistles, and Amber could see now that there were monsters coming for her, dark shapes all around, converging through the brush.

She had no hope of escape.

She could think of only one thing to do.

Sing.

* * *

"What are you doing out here?" the snake-eagle demanded of Ben.

Ben looked up, and he was so frightened that all eight of his legs were quivering and threatening to collapse.

"I just, I just came out for some sun," Ben said.

"Ticks don't crave sunlight," the monster said. "Ticks crave only warm blood."

Ben didn't know what to answer, and so he just stood there, trembling, afraid to move.

And then he heard singing—a familiar voice—in the woods behind him.

The trail is long and lonely,
And soon I'll reach the end,
In sunlight or in shadow,
I'll come to you, my friend.

Ben whirled and peered into the brush. It wasn't just a song, it was a song of warning and comfort.

Amber had come to save him!

The snake-eagle hissed and peered outside, then flapped its mighty wings. Ben was bowled over by the backwash as the air currents fanned him against the wall. Yet he scrabbled to his feet, peered out into the bright sunlight, and searched for Amber.

The snake-eagle rose high in the air, searching, searching, then let out a piercing cry and dove toward a bush. Ben saw Amber there, and he cried out in his small, tick's voice, "Amber, watch out!"

But as the snake-eagle dove, Amber ran out along a limb, hoisted her needle, and boldly waited. As the snake-eagle was about to hit her, she hurled her weapon with all of her might.

Ben couldn't tell exactly what happened, but he saw the needle whip through the air, a flash of silver blurring like a bullet, and then the snake-eagle screamed a mighty death cry that shook the very leaves of the trees and crashed into the smoking pool.

But in the brush all around Amber, Ben could see movement, strange creatures bowling through the underbrush. Horrible vines slithering in her direction. There was no way that she could hope to escape.

And so Ben stood there at the mouth of cave, in the full sunlight, and began to sing his loudest.

When death is at your doorway,
And there's no one to defend
In day or utter darkness,
I'll stand with you, my friend.

The shaking and slithering in the forest came to a halt as Amber's hunters became confused. Then Ben saw them reorient, and the monsters began racing through the Weird Wood toward him!

I'm going to die, he thought. But Ben felt good, proud. Vervane the vole had once asked him to sing his song, and an octopus had asked him to do so too. At the time, Ben had told them that he had no song.

But now he had found one.

Nightwing came whistling toward Amber, his voice sounding like fingernails on a chalkboard.

CHAPTER 20

THE MOUSE THAT ROARED

The fierce wind that carves a mighty mountain can also polish a diamond and thus reveal its inner light.
—Rufus Flycatcher

UNSURE WHAT TO DO, Ben stood with quivering legs until he heard a voice from the back of the cave.

"How quaint," Nightwing said. "My little blood-sucking parasite has a friend."

Ben whirled just as Nightwing came swooping out of the darkness and grabbed Ben with his gnarled feet.

Nightwing swept over the Weird Wood, swooping between bushes like an ace pilot, diving between the fork of two branches in a twisted pine, bursting through the leaves of a low-hanging vine.

Ben should have realized how good he was. A bat that can fly through a hailstorm without getting hit wouldn't think twice about flying through this twisted jungle. "I knew that she'd come back," Nightwing said, as if to a confidante. "She couldn't resist. Without you as her familiar, she's just another vermin."

Nightwing came whistling toward Amber, screeching in the daylight, his voice sounding like fingernails on a chalkboard.

Ben saw Amber on the ground, running for all she was worth. She'd lost her only weapon, and now she was darting blindly along a low trail.

She peered over her shoulder, saw Nightwing swooping above her, and dove sideways into some brush.

Nightwing overshot her position and swooped up into the air, doing a barrel roll as he hurtled back toward her.

"What do you think?" the bat said. "Shall I mush her with a dirt clod and turn her into a little statue that will only last until the next rain? Or shall we make a more permanent sculpture of her—a monument to her stupidity?"

"She's not stupid," Ben groused. "She just doesn't know anything."

Ben turned and began to climb through Nightwing's thick fur, all eight legs trembling.

"What are you doing?" Nightwing demanded.

"I'm hungry," Ben said. "Your blood. I smell it in your veins, Master. It calls to me."

Nightwing gave a simpering laugh as he soared over the brush pile where Amber had taken refuge. "Come to take your rightful place at last?"

Ben only grunted in midstride. But it wasn't his rightful place that he was after. He needed to distract the bat, and he could think of only one way to fight back. He would plunge his little needlelike mouth deep into the bat's flesh and sever his "juggler" vein!

But suddenly Amber was out in the open, trying to run from beneath the brush, and Nightwing hissed a curse. "You cannot fight me. I am the immortal, the mystical, Edgar. Allen. Poe!"

Amber was leaping over a large round stone, looking up over her shoulder toward Ben and Nightwing, when she began to scream.

Suddenly the stone beneath her feet began to melt, like butter, and Amber was melting with it, mushing into a creature half-mouse, half-stone.

She cried out in a wail of grief, and with all of his heart, Ben wished that he were still Amber's familiar, that his magic power might flow to her.

* * *

Amber glanced up as Nightwing's shadow passed overhead. He seemed huge for a bat, as big as all of the sky.

She was all out of magic. She'd felt the last of it drain from her when she killed the snake-eagle, hurling her needle into its eye.

And now, she knew that she would die. There were monsters everywhere in the Weird Wood. She could see them running from the mouth of the cave, could hear them converging on her from every direction.

Her only hope was to run madly, race through the brush, and hope that it was thick enough to slow her attackers.

She rushed through a patch of sunlight. There was a sandy brown stone beneath her, and as the bat hissed, Amber felt her feet giving way beneath her, sinking into the sediment, becoming one with the stone.

She tried to pull her knees up, to free herself, but she could feel her legs frozen, immovable. She was turning into rock! She could hear it, a sound like stones cracking and grating against one another, and she could feel it—the rock rising up above her knees, to her waist, climbing toward her chest.

Time seemed to stop. The bat was there above her, Ben desperately plunging his proboscis into the monster, as if it were a spear.

Nightwing was so sure of himself, so confident, that he flew with his eyes closed while his huge ears were swept forward.

No, Amber realized in a rush of insight. *He's not confident. He's flying by sound.*

The stone had risen to her chest by now and would soon be at her neck.

Amber did the only thing that she could think to do. With one last desperate hope, she roared, "Leave us alone!"

The sound that came out was louder than the whistle of a freight train. It blasted the brush and shook leaves from the trees. It bounced off the mountainside and hit the clouds, reverberating like a bell.

And it struck Nightwing like a cannonball.

The big-eared bat, navigating solely by sound, veered sharply and slammed into a tree, a tree whose branches looked like grasping arms, a tree whose trunk had knotholes that looked like eyes and another that looked like a gaping mouth, and whose leafless limbs looked like arms flailing uselessly at the sky.

There was the sound of snapping bones, and the bat flopped down in a broken heap, landing amid a wild cucumber bush whose trumpet-shaped flowers made little satisfied smacking sounds as vines and tendrils grabbed the bat and gently began tugging it down into the dirt at its roots.

A mist began to rise from under the bush, a black shadow of smoke that lengthened and grew, like an enormous dragon. And then the wind began to whisper through it, and the shadow was borne, like a captive, out to sea.

"We really did change the world."

CHAPTER 21

THE MOST BEAUTIFUL MOUSE IN THE WORLD

To be defeated, you must first give up.
—BUSHMASTER

BEN FELL TO THE GROUND and stood in a daze for a moment, his ears still ringing from Amber's sonic blast.

He peered about and saw monsters racing toward Amber.

But she just stood there, a creature made of stone, unmoving, uncaring. She had become a statue.

The monsters gathered around Amber, glaring at the little stone statue. There was the eelipede and Fanglorious, a skunk-leech and a scorpion-rat. From every direction, the monsters began to appear.

None of them spoke or growled.

With Nightwing gone, they seemed lost.

Ben scampered up to the stone statue.

Amber's head was twisted up, just in the way that it had been when she'd roared. Her mouth was open, and there was a frantic look in her eyes.

Ben climbed up on the statue, and tears came to his eyes.

"Now what's going to happen to me?" he said bitterly. "You can't just leave me here. Amber? Can you hear me?"

But Amber didn't move. She just stared up toward the morning sunlight, her stone eyes unblinking.

"I'm sorry," Ben said. "I'm sorry that I put you through so much. I'm sorry that I tried to feed you to the lizard. I'm sorry that I tried to leave you. Come back, Amber. Come back, and I'll stay with you. I'll help you free the mice of the world."

Amber remained still, unmoving.

Fanglorious growled, "She's dead, lad. They're all dead—them folks that got turned into rocks and trees. They're no more alive than . . . Nightwing."

Ben whirled on the snake. Here in the sunlight, the strange snake with vibrant colors painted along its side seemed obviously destined to be the new leader of SADIST.

"Do you know any magic?" Ben said. "Can you turn her back into a mouse? I could be your familiar."

But Fanglorious shook his head. "Aside from my strange coloration, there isn't anything magical about me."

Ben looked out over the other monsters. There was nothing special about any of them, he decided. They were just unfortunate critters who got caught in the wrong place at the wrong time.

Turning away, Ben began the long trek home. It was miles and miles to Dallas, Oregon. And he suspected that he'd never make it alive. He was already so hungry and tired that he didn't even think he could make it to the nearest freeway.

Still, there's a chance, he thought. I could go to the freeway and wait by the side of the road for some mountain biker to come along. Then all I have to do is hop on, get a drink, and hope that he takes me in the right direction.

But then what? Even if Ben made it home alive, what would he do? Crawl into his mother's messy house and live among the ants and the cockroaches until he grew old and died?

Yeah, Ben thought, *that's what I'll do.*

Ben hadn't taken more than a dozen steps when his legs got tangled and he tripped, falling on his face. He just lay there a moment, wishing that someone would step on him, when he felt something strange—a quivering in the ground. A pounding sound came once, then stopped, then rose again more loudly.

Just like on Jurassic Park, Ben thought. *A T-Rex is coming.*

He didn't move. The ground quivered again, and then the rumbling shook in earnest. It felt as if the whole world would tear apart. The trees were shaking, and the monsters roared in fear.

Ben staggered to his feet and peered around. The creatures were gaping about in terror and began to scream.

Ben was looking straight at the eelipede when it shrieked. One moment, there was a horrible monster in front of him, with armored plates on its back and a hundred oily feet, and the next there was a giant wolf eel slithering on the ground while a centipede crawled off.

The same happened with a nearby scorpion-rat. One moment, there was an evil creature squeaking in pain, thrashing its tail as if looking for something to poison, and the next moment there was a rat racing away from a tiny scorpion. Even Fanglorious was a strange snake one moment, and the next he was a common garter snake, slinking away, while next to him lay a Polaroid camera.

Is all of Nightwing's magic dying with him? Ben wondered. He glanced toward Amber and saw what looked like dust falling off of her.

Suddenly she breathed. She threw her tiny paws up in the sky and shouted to the creatures and the plants of the Weird Wood, "You're free! I free you all!"

And then Ben saw the truth: Amber was unmushing everything!

A nearby bush that had looked like some monster trapped in pain, suddenly turned into a crow and flapped into the sky. A tree became a deer that bounded away gracefully. And suddenly there were raccoons and squirrels and robins bolting from Shrew Hill in a wild stampede.

Amber whirled toward Ben. "Let's get out of here," she shouted, "before we get trampled by a herd of rampaging chipmunks!"

Just then, a crazed cottontail came leaping through the grass, and Amber ducked just in time to keep from getting squished.

Amber reached a paw out to Ben, and he went whisking toward her and landed with a plop on the soft fur of her belly.

"Hold on tight," she commanded him, and then added, "I wish we were at your house."

The effect of her wish was amazing. It was as if a bottle rocket exploded beneath Amber. One moment she was standing on the ground, and the next moment there was a hissing explosion, and she was hurtling through the air. The force of the wind buffeted Ben, and he clung tightly to her fur, but even eight legs didn't seem to be enough. He began to slip, and Amber reached down with a comforting paw and just held him in place.

Then they were whisking through the air, shooting over the endless forests, the hills and lakes, the winding rivers.

They picked up speed, and the wind became stronger, and suddenly it stopped altogether. They were going faster and faster, but it was as if there were a magical pocket of air that surrounded them. Ben realized that Amber must have wished for it.

"Did you mean what you said?" Amber asked. "Do you really want to stay a mouse and come with me to help free all of mousekind?"

Ben thought for a long moment. "I guess," he said, for he didn't have any other choice.

"I think that you're lying," Amber said. "I think that you really want to be a human."

"I don't know," Ben said honestly. "I wasn't very good at it."

"And I haven't been very good at being a mouse," Amber said. "At least . . . I wasn't good to you."

Ben thought back on all that had happened, on how Amber had come to save him, even if all that she could do was to act as a decoy and draw off his enemies. "You did pretty good at the end," Ben said.

Amber smiled.

"If I turned you back into a human," Amber asked, "could we still be friends?"

"Yeah," Ben said, growing excited at the thought. "I could even help you. I could take you to pet shops and help you free the mice. And then we could let them live in the backyard, and I'd bring lots of food for them, and . . ." the thought trailed off. "But you can't turn me back into a human. You can't cast a spell that's a lie."

"You're right," Amber said. "I didn't want you to be a human because I thought that it meant that I would lose you. But . . . I think I know a way." Amber sniffed.

Ben looked up and saw that Amber was crying.

Suddenly there was a jolt, and they began to slow, as if they were in a car that was running out of gas. They shuddered, and Ben looked down. They were dropping toward Ben's backyard.

"Hold on," Amber said. "I think you're running out of magic."

They sputtered and began to fall, and just as they neared the ground, Amber seemed to get her magic back, and they spurted the last few yards over the huge pine trees and housetops, over the cars and yards.

And then they were there, falling with a thud among the wildflowers and deep grass.

Against all hopes, Ben found himself home, and a profound sense of gratitude welled up in him.

"Ben," Amber said. "Close your eyes. And keep them closed for a minute."

"Why?" he started to say, but it just came out as a grunt. He closed his eyes.

"Now," Amber said, "let's see if I can do this right."

She reached down, stroked Ben's head and back, and then stepped away a few paces. Ben sat in the sunlight, letting it bounce on his head. In the distance he could hear the slamming of a car door as the neighbor headed for work, and from the fields across the street came the song of a meadowlark.

"Ben," Amber said sincerely. "I wish that we could see what it would be like to be human."

Then it happened. Ben felt no pain this time. Only a twinge really, as his extra four legs began to shrink away.

His front legs turned into arms, and he could feel himself rising, rising, his hands and feet all on the ground, until he straightened up and stood.

He just held still, quivering in the sunlight, rejoicing in the sensation of being human—in feeling the cool morning wind blowing on his arms and face. He hadn't felt that in days—not as a mouse, insulated by fur, or even as a tick, insulated by a carapace.

"You can open your eyes now," Amber said, and Ben looked down and saw the bare feet of a young woman. She wore a simple dress that looked like a print stolen straight from the backyard—stalks of grass, buttercups and daisies, dried coneflowers and Indian tobacco.

And as Ben looked up into her face, he gasped. Amber stood before him, transformed. She was, Ben realized, the most beautiful girl that he had ever seen. Her hair was a strange brownish gray. Mouse-colored, he realized. And her eyes were black and sparkling.

"Amber?" Ben asked in amazement.

She nodded. "We're low on magic. This won't last. But I think that when we've got enough power again, I can wish that you are human, as long as I'm human too."

"Wow," Ben said.

Had Amber been that pretty as a mouse? Ben wondered. And in his heart he knew the answer. Of course she had been that pretty. That's why he had picked her from the pet shop.

But what now? he wondered. *What would I do with her? Where would she live?*

He imagined her living like a wild creature in the woods up above the house, somewhere near

Bushmaster's burrow. But then he thought, *No, she'll be a human now. She'll need a house, and I'll need to take her to school with me.*

He imagined keeping her in the attic where Mom and Dad never went. She could use magic to feed herself, and they could go everywhere together, freeing the mice of the world.

And even as he stood there, imagining what the future might bring, he began to shrink again.

In moments, he was small again. As small as a mouse.

He heard a yowl.

The sound of a cat wouldn't even have registered a week ago, but Ben nearly jumped out of his skin. He whirled, and saw the white body and black spots that identified Domino.

The cat was fleeing in a wild panic, and right behind him, tripping and leaping, half a dozen mice and voles gave chase, all of them armed with needles.

He could almost imagine the news headlines now, as word got out that the mice of Dallas, Oregon, had armed themselves.

"We've already changed the world," Amber said, her black eyes peering at him from dark fur. "Maybe more than either one of us has realized. Maybe that's all that I really need to do—teach the mice of the world how to free themselves."

Ben glanced back toward the house and thought of going home. He noticed that there was a mass of black objects spilling out the back door of the garage. Flies. Dead flies.

And he remembered the spider who'd said that the odds against him getting out of the pet shop alive were a million to one.

A million greenbottle flies! Ben thought. *Looks like he collected on the bet*.

"We really did change the world," Ben said, shaking his head in wonder. He looked at the flies and imagined trying to clean out the garage with a shovel. That was one mess that he didn't ever want to pick up, even if he had to leave it for his mother.

Then he turned away, and he and Amber went hopping toward Bushmaster's hole beneath the pine—hop, stop, and look.

And for the moment, Ben was grateful just to be a mouse again.